☞ **W9-BYH-320**

# THE
# HIGHLY TRAINED
# DOGS
## OF PROFESSOR
# PETIT

# THE HIGHLY TRAINED DOGS OF PROFESSOR PETIT

### BY

## CAROL RYRIE BRINK

two lions

two lions

This is a work of fiction. Names, characters, organizations, places, events, and incidents are either products of the author's imagination or are used fictitiously.

Text copyright © 1953 Carol Ryrie Brink
Introduction copyright © 2015 Nancy Pearl
All rights reserved.

No part of this book may be reproduced, or stored in a retrieval system, or transmitted in any form or by any means, electronic, mechanical, photocopying, recording, or otherwise, without express written permission of the publisher.

Published by Two Lions, New York

www.apub.com

Amazon, the Amazon logo, and Two Lions are trademarks of Amazon.com, Inc., or its affiliates.

ISBN-13: 9781503945197 (hardcover)
ISBN-10: 1503945197 (hardcover)
ISBN-13: 9781503945203 (paperback)
ISBN-10: 1503945200 (paperback)

Book design by Virginia Pope

Printed in the United States of America

*For Anne and Scotty,*
*and their dogs Tiger and Troubles,*
*with love.*

# CONTENTS

# INTRODUCTION

# NANCY PEARL

Carol Ryrie Brink (1895–1980) was a highly prolific writer who penned well-reviewed and immensely interesting books for both children and adult readers. Yet not only are most of her books long out of print and generally forgotten, she's basically known today for only one particular novel, *Caddie Woodlawn*. It won the 1936 John Newbery Award, the highest honor bestowed by the American Library Association for a work of fiction or nonfiction for young readers, and it brought her enduring fame.

Brink was born in the small university town of Moscow, Idaho, and if you go to the public library there today you will not only see a painting of the author, but you'll discover that the children's area is named after her, The Carol Ryrie Brink Reading Room.

*The Highly Trained Dogs of Professor Petit* was originally published in 1953. Miss Whitehead, the librarian at the public library nearest to my house in Detroit, knew me well. She understood that all I really wanted to read at age nine or ten were either books about dogs and horses or mysteries. She always had a couple of books to give to me each time I saw her, and I remember her saying as she handed me a copy of Mrs. Brink's book, "Well, Nancy, you've hit the jackpot this time. This is a book that's both about dogs—wonderful, amazing dogs—and a mystery that only one of the dogs can solve."

As you might imagine, I was immediately hooked. I couldn't wait to find out what happened in *The Highly Trained Dogs of Professor Petit* and began reading it as I walked home from the library and finished it later that night. Then I immediately started it again. Miss Whitehead was right: this is a perfect choice for any child, like the child I was, who loves mysteries and/or books about dogs.

In Brink's novel, which takes place in 1852, eleven-year-old Willie is brought to Puddling Center from the country to help out his very stern uncle, Postmaster Scrivens. One day, while running an errand for Uncle Scrivens, Willie meets Professor Petit, who travels around in a covered wagon putting on shows with his five highly trained dogs—Sancho, Prince, Grushenka, Liddy, and Tip. Amazingly enough, Sancho, the very smartest of these very smart dogs, cannot only spell his own name but other short words like *dog* and *cat* and *man* out of alphabet blocks. And he can talk!

But Professor Petit and his highly trained dogs find their livelihood is threatened because a traveling circus run by Hulk Hoskins not only features a dog named Brutus, but a real, live tiger who jumps through a hoop of fire! How will Professor Petit's show survive? Even while they're worrying about that, Willie and Professor Petit learn that Sancho is apparently responsible for a terrible act of violence. Can Willie discover the real culprit? Of course I shared *The Highly Trained Dogs of Professor Petit* with my children, who loved this timeless mystery starring dogs as much as I did. I hope you, or the children in your life, enjoy it as much as we all did.

—*Nancy Pearl*

# MEETING IN THE WOODS

There were really not enough boys in Puddling Center in the year 1852 to do all the work that usually falls to boys to do. Puddling Center was small, but the crop of local boys was smaller. The people of Puddling Center were serious people. They did not laugh or sing or dance. They liked to see that everything was seriously and promptly done. Without a good, handy errand boy, they found it difficult to get along.

Postmaster Scrivens, who was perhaps the most serious of all the serious people in Puddling Center, gave the matter some serious thought. He remembered that his sister Sara, who lived on a farm near Wickersham, had seven children.

"I will write to Sara," he said, "and ask her if she will lend us one of her boys."

In a few days, Postmaster Scrivens had a reply from his sister Sara. She was willing to lend him her son Willie, who was the fourth from each end of the seven children. In fact, the bearer of the letter was none other than Willie himself, with all of his clothing in a small sack on his back. He was prepared to stay.

Willie was a bright boy of eleven years who could do a great many things. There were a great many things in Puddling Center to do, as Willie soon found out.

At home Willie had led an idle, pleasant life. The family dog liked Willie better than any of the other children, and together they had roamed the woods and fields, fishing, watching the little wild animals and bugs, or looking up at the clouds that sailed in the sky. The people at home liked to sing and laugh and dance.

Willie found Puddling Center quite different. First of all he missed old Sport, the dog, and next he missed his pleasant, idle time. The days were not long enough in Puddling Center. He had to carry letters into the country for his uncle. He had to pull the baker's cart to deliver the baker's bread. He had to take the farmer's sheep to pasture and bring them home again at night. Besides all this, the weaver expected Willie to be on hand to chase after the balls of yarn when they dropped down and rolled away, and the miller expected Willie to kill or capture the rats and mice that stole the grain in the mill. When he had done all of these things, if there was any time left over, Willie was expected to go to school.

The strange thing about it was that Willie really wanted to go to school. The prospect of going to school and learning all sorts of interesting things had made him eager to come to Puddling Center. But now that he was here, his many jobs kept him busy all day long. The baker, the farmer, the weaver, the miller, each paid Willie a little money for the work he did. His uncle Scrivens gave him his room and board and a shilling a week.

"Willie," his uncle Scrivens said, "someday you are going to be rich."

"But what is the use of being rich," Willie asked, "if I don't know anything?"

"Tomfoolery!" said Uncle Scrivens. "Anyone who knows how to become rich knows all that he needs to know."

Willie wondered if this were true. He did not think so. But it was impossible to argue with Uncle Scrivens, because arguing made Uncle Scrivens angry and wasted too much time.

Before the day had fairly begun, Willie was often tired out. A little pleasure now and then might have made him less tired. But Postmaster Scrivens did not understand that.

"Keep a boy busy," Uncle Scrivens said, "and you keep him out of mischief."

One day when he saw Willie stopping for a moment to read a circus poster that was stuck on the post office wall, Mr. Scrivens was quite impatient.

"Willie," he said, "you are wasting a moment of your time! Here I am, giving one of my poor dear sister's seven children a wonderful opportunity to get rich, and what do you do in return? You stand there looking at a picture of a tiger jumping through a flaming hoop. Hoskins's Circus, indeed! Be off with you, and deliver that letter. The baker and the farmer and the weaver and the miller are all waiting for you. Be off, Willie! Be off!"

Willie ran off as fast as he could go. But he had never seen a circus nor a tiger, and he couldn't help thinking how exciting it was that Hoskins's Circus was coming to town.

*If only I can find time to go!* Willie thought. *But, if there isn't time to go to school, sure as shooting there won't be time to go to the circus.*

It was a beautiful summer morning and Willie had a long way to walk into the country to deliver his letter. He jogged along happily, thinking that if only old Sport had been with him, life would not be bad at all today. When he had delivered the letter, the man to whom it was addressed said, "Did you come by the highway, Willie?"

Willie nodded.

"Then let me tell you," said the man, "that by taking the little woods road that branches to the left, you will save yourself a mile and get back to Puddling Center a half an hour earlier."

"Thank you," Willie said. For a moment he wondered if he really wanted to get back to Puddling Center a half an hour earlier than Uncle Scrivens expected him. But then he decided that it would show Uncle Scrivens what good intentions he had.

The woods road unrolled pleasantly among the trees. Birds sang, and daisies and buttercups bloomed. The air was sweet and clear. Willie smelled birch smoke and the wonderful odor of frying bacon. He remembered then that he had gone off without his breakfast. Uncle Scrivens had been in such a hurry to have the letter delivered that a slice of bread had been all Willie had taken time to eat.

Now, as Willie rounded a bend in the woods, he saw that the road opened out at this point into a sunny clearing. In the clearing a man in his shirt sleeves was cooking bacon and porridge over an open fire. But there were other strange and interesting things in the clearing, and Willie stopped in his tracks and stood there for a moment, just looking.

First of all, drawn up beside the road, was a small green caravan or covered wagon with windows in it, and a door at the back. Beyond the caravan a red roan pony was grazing among the buttercups and grasses. A clothesline had been strung out from the caravan to a nearby tree, and upon it fluttered and bobbed an odd assortment of clothing. There was a scarlet, long-tailed coat that probably belonged to the man who was frying the bacon. Beyond the coat there were five very small jackets of various colors and cuts, a large white ruffle, a dunce cap, two ballerina skirts, and three pairs of very small, brightly colored trousers. The curious thing about the trousers was that each and every pair had a small round hole in the back, as if for a tail to come through.

There was a curious sound here, too. From inside the caravan came a sound that was not quite singing and not quite barking and not quite howling and not quite yodeling. But it was something like each of these things. Sometimes the sound was high and sometimes low. Now it seemed that someone inside the caravan might possibly be practicing scales for a singing lesson. Yet it was not exactly that either.

The pony paid no attention to the strange sounds in the caravan and neither did the man by the fire. They seemed to think that everything was as it should be. The man looked sad, Willie thought, although it was hard to understand why anyone should be sad on such a lovely day and with bacon sizzling in a pan.

Willie began to walk slowly toward the caravan and the fire. His feet made a quiet sound of walking on the rutted road.

Suddenly the noises from the caravan completely changed. They burst out loudly now. *Yap-yap-yap! Bow-wow-wow!* and *Arff! arff! arff!* in several different tones of voice, but all unmistakably the voices of dogs, giving the alarm.

The pony went on munching buttercups, but the man at the fire looked around.

"Tut! tut!" he said severely. "You've disturbed the morning practice hour, my boy."

"I'm very sorry, sir," Willie said. "I was just going by. I didn't mean to do anything."

"'I didn't mean to' never built a tower," the man said. With which puzzling remark, he balanced the frying pan on a flat stone near the fire, arose, and came briskly forward. He was not a large man but a very brisk one. His face was slightly foreign-looking.

He had a reassuring twinkle in his eye, and the lips, under a brisk black moustache, smiled engagingly. Willie liked him.

"It doesn't really matter," the man said, speaking loudly to make himself heard above the uproar of barking. "Time's about up anyway, and there's no use practicing with nothing to look forward to. A business with no future! Too bad! Indeed, too bad!"

He went around to the back of the caravan and opened the door. Five dogs leaped out of it, barking and jumping and wagging their tails like mad.

"Wheesht! Wheesht!" the little man said, holding up his hand. "It's only a boy, friends. No cause for excitement. Steady now."

The five dogs stopped barking and sat down in a semicircle before the man, with their tails curled up expectantly behind them. Their tongues lolled out of their mouths in mirth and excitement. They rolled their eyes curiously toward Willie and then back again to their master.

"Now," said he, "be civil to the boy, won't you? You've scared him out of his wits."

"Oh, no, sir!" Willie cried. "Excuse me, sir, but I've never been scared by a dog."

"Ah!" said the man, looking at Willie with new interest. "Never scared? *Never?*"

"I figure it this way," Willie said. "Dogs usually want to be friends. If they see that you are scared or don't like them, then sometimes they'll be mean. But, if you like them, they're sure to be good-natured."

"Ah-hah!" cried the man. "A wise boy! A boy after my own heart! You have discovered one of the universal laws of nature, son!"

"I don't know about that," said Willie doubtfully. "But dogs—I like them."

"Splendid!" the man said. "It's enough to make us all friends, eh, children?"

The dogs began to frisk and bark, this time with pure pleasure. They came up and sniffed around Willie. One of them licked his hand, and then, to his great surprise, one of them sat up in front of him, and another lay down and rolled over. The smallest of the dogs stood on his hind legs and pulled Willie's handkerchief out of his pocket. He was about to run away with it, when his master cried: *"Tip!"* in a very stern voice. The small dog returned and dropped Willie's handkerchief before him as if in a game of Drop the Handkerchief.

"Tut! tut!" said the man. "No tricks now! Breakfast first. Will you join us, boy? We haven't much to offer today, but we are never too poor to share with a friend."

Willie thought of Uncle Scrivens. But, by taking the woods road, he had gained a half an hour. He could eat breakfast in this delightful company and still arrive back at the post office as soon as Uncle Scrivens expected him.

"I'd be more than pleased," said Willie.

As he came around the caravan, he saw that a sign was painted on the side of it.

*Professor Petit*
*and*
*His Highly Trained Dogs*

# THE HIGHLY TRAINED DOGS

As Willie followed Professor Petit around the caravan, his heart had begun to pound with excitement.

"Excuse me, sir," he said, "but are you a part of Hoskins's Circus?"

"Why, no," said Professor Petit. His face suddenly darkened and grew sad. It was as if a cloud had passed across the sun. "What makes you ask a thing like that?"

"Well," said Willie, "I saw a poster of Hoskins's Circus. It's soon to come to town, and I just thought—. Hoskins has a tiger, sir. It jumps through a flaming hoop."

"Yes," said Professor Petit, "Hulk Hoskins has a tiger. It's Hoskins's tiger that has ruined us, isn't it, my friends?"

Thus appealed to, the dogs all barked in agreement, but Willie could see that their attention was really fixed upon the bacon in the pan and the oatmeal porridge that stood near it.

"I guess I don't quite understand," said Willie.

"I will tell you," said Professor Petit. As he spoke, he dished out the bacon and porridge into a large pan for the five dogs and into two small dishes for Willie and himself. The dogs stood around the large pan without quarrelling, waving their tails with enjoyment as they ate. Willie, too, spooned up his food with relish. It had a pleasant tang of wood smoke, and the savor that only food eaten out of doors can have. But, although he had given himself a very small helping, Professor Petit seemed to lack appetite for his food.

"Hoskins's Circus has ruined us," he said sadly. "Once we were the most popular show on the road. Everybody came to see my highly trained dogs. I cannot tell you what skill, what patience, what understanding and devotion I have put into the training of my dogs. I do not hesitate to say that they are the most highly trained dogs in the world. About a year ago another animal show appeared upon the road, Hoskins's Show. The animals performed only the very simplest of tricks and those to the tune of a cracking whip. The poor things were afraid for their lives. There was a frightened bear who did a kind of shuffling dance at one end of a chain. There was a dog, Brutus, who performed certain feats of strength, such as hanging onto a strap while he was pulled upward by a rope. But they had none of the skills that my dogs possess, of walking the tightrope, climbing ladders, and talking."

"*Talking?*" cried Willie in surprise.

"Why, certainly," said Professor Petit. "Sancho, come here, my boy."

The black shaggy dog with the curly tail detached himself reluctantly from the breakfast pan and trotted up to his master. Professor Petit put his hand gently on Sancho's throat, and said, "Speak, boy! *Speak!*"

"How are you, my friend?" said the dog, or so it certainly sounded to Willie.

"Very good," said the professor. "Now finish your breakfast, boy." The dog wagged his tail and returned to the pan of food.

Willie was openmouthed with astonishment. He forgot to eat. He could hardly speak for wonder and surprise. But Professor Petit went on with his story, as if nothing out of the ordinary had taken place.

"Hoskins has nothing to compare with that," he said. "He trains his animals with fear and not with kindness. It is impolite for me to speak ill of a rival, but the truth compels me to say that Hulk Hoskins is a cruel and dishonest man. At first we had nothing to fear from him, for his show was decidedly inferior to ours. And then last winter in some way that I do not know about, he was able to secure a tiger for his show. Have you ever seen a tiger, my boy?"

"No," Willie said, "that's why I wanted to go to Hoskins's Circus, to see a real, live tiger."

"Exactly," said Professor Petit. "To see a real, live tiger! Everyone wants to see the tiger. Hoskins had all of these beautiful posters printed with colored pictures of the tiger. He sent them to all of the postmasters in the region and asked to have them posted on the town walls. Now people are only interested in seeing tigers. They say to themselves that anybody can see dogs. Every town is full of dogs. The people will not pay out their money to look at dogs, when, by waiting a few days, they can see a tiger. It is too bad, but our business has been completely ruined. We play to empty seats. I don't mind telling you that this is the last good meal we are likely to have, unless something can be done. And you say that Hoskins's Circus is coming to your town, too? How soon?"

"In just a few days," said Willie. "On Saturday, I believe."

"Then we are finished," said Professor Petit. "I

thought that by coming here to this rural region, I might get away from Hoskins and his tiger. But I seem to have run directly into his path."

"Isn't there anything you can do?" asked Willie. "A talking dog now—that's really something!"

"We can only go on as we have been doing," said Professor Petit, "giving honest entertainment and hoping for the best. If times are bad, we go a little hungry. The pony can always eat grass by the wayside, but the dogs and I must have meat and porridge. If the worst comes to the worst, I can always give up showing my dogs and go to work for a farmer to earn our living."

"But couldn't the dogs hunt?" asked Willie. "If they could catch rabbits and squirrels, they'd get enough to eat."

"I have thought of that," said Professor Petit. "Liddy, the fox terrier, is very good at catching rats and mice. But rats and mice are destructive creatures whereas rabbits and squirrels are generally good and gentle animals. My dogs have been highly educated. I think it would be disagreeable to them to live by killing their fellow creatures."

"Rats and mice," said Willie thoughtfully. "The miller could use—"

"Of course," said Professor Petit sadly, "one learns

to overcome his scruples in a hard world, I find. But it would break my heart to see my highly trained dogs wasting their education by returning to a state of savagery."

The thought of the miller had reminded Willie that he had better hurry back to Puddling Center. But it was very hard to tear himself away.

The dogs had polished off the last morsel of food in their pan, and they came and stood around Professor Petit as if they would enjoy eating a little more.

"I'm sorry, my friends," said Professor Petit. "At present there is no more, but have courage, for perhaps today our fortunes may take a better turn."

Willie was sorry that he had eaten any part of the breakfast now that he knew it to be their last. He put his hand in his pocket and drew out a couple of shillings.

"I would like you to have these, sir, to buy food for the dogs. My trouble is just the opposite from yours. For you have education and no work or money, whilst I have a little money and so much work that I don't find any time to go to school and get an education."

"How strange!" said Professor Petit. "But, my dear lad, I cannot accept your money unless you will let us give you a show."

At the word "show," the dogs began to leap about and bark. The largest dog, whose name was Prince, ran to the clothesline, and, jumping up, caught it in his teeth and shook it, so that all of the strange and brightly colored garments fell onto the grass. Each dog ran and caught up a jacket or a pair of trousers in his mouth. They crowded around Professor Petit, wagging their tails and begging to begin.

Professor Petit put on his scarlet coat and helped the five dogs into their costumes. Willie had never seen such an amazing sight in his life.

Sancho, the black, shaggy dog with the curly tail, wore a scarlet jacket and yellow trousers. Prince, the large brindle boxer, wore orange and green. Grushenka, who was also a boxer, but smaller than Prince and of a beautiful fawn color, wore a light-blue jacket and a ballerina skirt. Liddy, the fox terrier, also wore a ballerina skirt and a little purple jacket with a plumed bonnet on her head. Her sharp, pointed nose stuck out of the bonnet in a very comical way. The fifth dog, Tip, was the one who had pulled Willie's handkerchief out of his pocket. He was very short in the legs and long in the body. He was yellow with a black spot over one eye and a black tip on the end of his tail. He wore a clown suit with a ruffle about his neck. The dunce cap seemed to belong to him.

Willie sat on the grass beside the caravan and watched the highly trained dogs of Professor Petit perform their tricks.

Professor Petit did not use a whip, but only spoke to his dogs in a reasonable tone of voice, and they seemed to delight in giving a performance.

In several numbers the dogs all performed together. Standing on their hind legs, they waltzed in couples to a tune which the professor played on a jaw harp. Liddy and Sancho waltzed together, and so did the two boxers. Then they sat on their hind legs and sang together to the professor's music. Willie realized that the sound he had heard coming from the caravan earlier in the morning had been a rehearsal for their singing.

Each dog, however, had his or her own special skill. Prince was very strong. He could carry Liddy in a basket in his mouth. He could parade on his hind legs with a wooden gun on his shoulder. He could jump over hurdles or a stick held as high as the professor's head.

Grushenka was clever with a ball. She could balance it on her nose, toss it up into the air, and catch it in her mouth as it came down.

Liddy could climb a small ladder on her hind legs, walk across a tightrope that was stretched between two ladders, and go down the other ladder on her front legs with her hind legs up in the air.

But Sancho was the most sagacious of all the dogs. He not only knew how to speak, but he had learned to spell. Professor Petit put before him a row of twenty-six little wooden blocks on each of which was printed a letter of the alphabet.

"What is your name?" he asked, and the black dog quickly picked out six letters with his paw, took them in his mouth, and arranged them in order so that they spelled S A N C H O. He could also spell D O G and C A T and M A N. There were numbers on the other side of some of the blocks, and, when Professor Petit asked Sancho how old he was, the dog pulled out the block with the number 3 on it.

"How many highly trained dogs do I have?" asked the professor.

Sancho picked out the number 5.

"Now, let us see if you can add," said Professor Petit. "Add two and two, and how many will you have?"

The block that Sancho chose said 4.

"Very well. Then subtract 3 from 4. How many are left?"

Sancho selected the number 1.

Willie was perfectly amazed. "Does he really understand what he is doing, Professor?"

"Well," said Professor Petit, "I think that he does. I have taught him, of course, just which block belongs with which question. He understands the tone of my voice and the position of the block. But I often wonder, if I should ask him a question that we have never rehearsed, wouldn't he be able to answer it? He is an extremely sagacious dog. I have often wondered."

"And when he *speaks*—?" continued Willie.

At the sound of the word *speak*, Sancho said, "How are you, my friend?"

It was not, perhaps, as clear as the first time Willie had heard him say it. Professor Petit explained that this was because Sancho had said it alone, without any help. "You see," said the professor, "when I put my fingers on his throat, I can manipulate the vocal cords in such a way that the sound comes out quite clearly. But he has learned to make the sounds almost as well by himself. Every day he does it better."

"How did you ever think of teaching him to talk?" asked Willie.

"It has always been an ambition of mine," replied the professor, "to find an animal who would be intelligent enough to cooperate with me in this way. A few years ago, I was told that Mr. Ruskin, who is a well-known English author, had trained his pet dog to say, 'How are you, Grandmama?' He did so by pressing gently on the dog's vocal cords when the dog whined or barked. Sancho was a puppy at that time, and I saw that he was intelligent and eager to learn. I thought that whatever Mr. Ruskin could do with a dog, Professor Petit could also do. However, since we had no grandmama in our troupe, I thought it better to teach him to ask after the health of a friend. So there you have it!"

"Can he say anything else?" asked Willie.

"No, but he can sing and he can yodel. A truly remarkable dog!"

Now, throughout this performance, Willie had noticed that the little yellow dog named Tip was very cheerful and active, but that he never seemed to do things in exactly the right way. When the other dogs waltzed, Tip walked on his front feet with his hind legs in the air. When the other dogs jumped hurdles, he ran under the hurdles instead of leaping over them. When the other dogs climbed ladders, Tip lay down and pretended to be dead. Professor Petit put Tip upon a stool with a dunce cap on his head; but, when they were not looking, he jumped down and began to roll over.

"What is Tip's special trick?" Willie asked.

"Alas!" said Professor Petit. "Tip is our dunce and

# INTERRUPTED PERFORMANCE

On the way back to Puddling Center, Willie could think of nothing but Professor Petit's Highly Trained Dogs. Life had suddenly become very interesting for Willie. He whistled as he ran, took several shortcuts across fields, and when he came to a fence, he vaulted over it, almost as beautifully as Prince would have done.

Willie had promised the professor that he would tell everyone in town about the dogs and try to get a good crowd out to see the show the next afternoon. He had forgotten how late he must be until he saw the post office looming up ahead of him. In the doorway stood Uncle Scrivens, with a face like a thundercloud.

"Late!" Uncle Scrivens said. "Late again! Now you will have to run all day to catch up. No time for school today."

"I'm sorry, Uncle," said Willie, "but I have just seen a most wonderful sight. I couldn't hurry. Five educated dogs, I saw. And, would you believe it? One of them can speak words. They are going to give a show here in town tomorrow afternoon. You must go, Uncle Scrivens. You really must."

"You have been wasting your time, Willie," said Uncle Scrivens severely. "And, as for shows, anyone can see dogs, but I shall wait for the *tiger*."

Willie had much the same response from the baker, the farmer, the weaver, and the miller. They had all seen the posters of Hoskins's Circus, and they were determined to save their money and wait for the tiger.

Willie rushed through his work as fast as he could. He hurried to the schoolhouse, just as the children were being dismissed for the day. Most of the pupils were girls, or boys too small to do errands, but all of them liked Willie and were sorry that he could not find time to go to school. They crowded around him now and listened while he told them about Professor Petit's dogs. "We will ask our parents if we may go to see Professor Petit's show," they said.

"And you are sure you wouldn't rather see the tiger?" Willie asked. Because he did not want them to feel cheated later.

The children thought about this. They talked

it over among themselves. "A tiger? Or five highly trained dogs?" It was a hard decision to make. "Perhaps we can see both," someone said. Someone else said, "Even if we can't see both, dogs are more fun than tigers." It is true that children are always partial to dogs.

That evening before sundown, the green caravan came driving into town. The red roan pony trotted proudly, pulling the caravan. Professor Petit sat upon the driver's seat, resplendent in his scarlet coat. Inside the caravan, the dogs barked.

There was a large public square in Puddling Center with trees and benches. On one side of the square was the church, on another was the courthouse, on another were the post office and the shops. The fourth side looked out toward the river and the mill. Professor Petit and his dogs made their camp for the night on the edge of the square beside the river. With Willie's shillings they bought four large loaves of bread from the baker, and so they were not hungry.

Until their mothers called them to bed, the school children came and stood around to watch the green caravan and the wonderful dogs. Willie was there, too, of course, for the dogs already considered him an old friend.

Even Uncle Scrivens came down to look the caravan over. But he was not very polite. He sniffed at the antics of the dogs, and he said to Professor Petit, "Where is your tiger?"

"Nevertheless," Willie told the professor, "I believe that you will have a pretty good crowd tomorrow. The children have promised to come. I wish that I could come, too. But I am afraid I'll never get through with all of my work in time."

"My dear boy," said Professor Petit, "do you mean to say that you cannot hurry through your work by noon on one special day of the year? Won't your uncle excuse you?"

"I'm afraid not," Willie said. "He never has. And there is so much to do that as soon as I finish one job, they've got another ready for me."

"Well, in that case," said the professor, "there is only one thing to do. My highly trained dogs must help you. If you all work together, the work will be done in a twinkle, eh, friends?" Thus appealed to, the dogs all began to bark in joyous assent.

It was a perfectly wonderful morning for Willie. Prince pulled the baker's cart for him, and Willie did not even have to go into the houses with the loaves of bread. The children and the housewives all came running out to get their bread from the cart, so that they could see the wonderful dog that pulled it.

Sancho went with Willie to the farmer's, and he was so skillful at herding the sheep and driving the cows that they were driven to pasture in half the time it usually took for Willie to do it. "I believe that Sancho could do it all alone," Willie said to himself, "now that he knows the way."

In the meantime Grushenka had gone to the weaver's, where she caught the balls of yarn when they fell from the bench or the loom, and tossed them back to the weaver before he had begun to miss them. The flying shuttles filled her with excitement, and if one happened to slip out of the weaver's hand, Grushenka caught it and instantly brought it back to him. The weaver was delighted.

Liddy had been sent to the miller's, where she spent a lively morning chasing the rats and mice. "My faith!" said the miller, "a dog is better than a boy at this business! Had I such a dog as Liddy, there would be no more varmints within a half mile of my mill."

Tip was the only dog who did not spend a useful morning. He lay in the sun with his nose on his paws. Whenever a fly came near him, he waved it away with his black-tipped tail, but without opening his eyes. "Alas!" said Professor Petit. He shook his head sadly at the sight of Tip's laziness. Just before dinner, however, Tip disappeared for a few moments on business of his own. When he returned he was carrying by the neck a nicely dressed fowl, which he laid with pride at his master's feet.

"Tip! Tip!" cried Professor Petit in a despairing voice, "how often must I warn you against taking what does not belong to you? I shall have to return this fowl to the butcher myself. Tip is the only one of my dogs who does not understand that a highly trained dog respects other people's property."

"Do you mean to say that he is a thief?" asked Willie.

"That is putting it a trifle harshly," said the professor. "The truth is that uneducated dogs have no sense of property. They take whatever they want whenever they can get it. I regret that Tip, in spite of my training, often behaves like an uneducated dog."

Besides introducing the dogs to their work, Willie had a number of letters to deliver. But by afternoon even Uncle Scrivens could not think of a thing for Willie to do that had not been done.

"Yes, Willie," Uncle Scrivens said reluctantly, "you may go to the dog show if your heart is set on it. But personally I think you are foolish not to save your money for the tiger."

Professor Petit had been busy in the square that morning setting up the ladders and the tightrope, the hurdles and the hoops. He had also set up a small house with windows and doors and a wide red chimney. It was something like a doll's house, but larger. In fact, it was of a perfect size for dogs, walking on their hind legs, to occupy.

The professor had spent some time in grooming the pony, and preparing for him a plumed bridle and a kind of platform that fitted on the pony's back like a saddle. A small red cart with ladders and hose like a fire wagon had also come out of the caravan.

Willie guessed, with delight, that there was more to the professor's show than he had seen the day before. He could hardly wait for the performance to begin.

By half past two in the afternoon, the children came marching, two by two, down from the schoolhouse with Miss Charmian, the teacher, behind them. They had persuaded her that it would be very educational for them to see Professor Petit's Highly Trained Dogs, and so she had excused school for the rest of the afternoon. A great many parents came, too. The farmer, the baker, the weaver, and the miller had been so pleased with the work done by the dogs in the morning that they also came, in spite of Hoskins's tiger. Only Uncle Scrivens shut himself up in the post office and refused to come.

"Hoskins's show is in the next town," he said. "It will be here tomorrow."

"Well, tomorrow is another day," said Willie cheerfully.

Willie helped Professor Petit by selling tickets, and he was delighted to see how gaily the shillings rolled into the empty money bag. It looked as if Professor Petit's troubles were over at last.

The show started very well with the entrance of the roan pony, trotting proudly and holding his head high. Behind him ran the five dogs, without their costumes. As the pony trotted around in a large circle, the dogs took turns leaping onto the platform on his back and off the other side. The professor stood by the ring and held out a large hoop. As the pony trotted by, the dog, who happened to be on the platform, would jump through the hoop and return to the back of the trotting pony. Only Tip was too short-legged and untrained to jump on the pony's back. But he ran in and out between the pony's legs and then played dead in the center of the ring.

After a few moments of this, Professor Petit and all of the dogs, except Prince, disappeared from the scene. Willie understood that they had gone behind the little house to get on their costumes, while Prince continued to entertain the audience by making prodigious leaps over the pony's back.

While all of this was going on, Willie happened to look around, and saw that a stranger had joined the edge of the crowd. He was a very large man with long black hair and heavy brows. In his ears there were shining hoops of gold. Beside him, held by a leash, was a large grey dog. Willie had never seen man or dog before, but instantly he knew who they must be. Professor Petit had said that Hulk Hoskins had a dog named Brutus, and on the dog's wide collar, for everyone to see, was the name *Brutus*, spelled out very clearly in copper nailheads. For a moment Willie was worried. But then he heard the children saying, "Oh!" and "Ah!", and he forgot about the strangers in watching Prince make even higher and finer leaps over the back of the pony.

Now Professor Petit's whistle blew, and the pony trotted away with Prince on his back. Prince jumped down and ran behind the little house, and Willie knew that the professor would be helping him into his coat and trousers. In the meantime the front door of the house opened, and out walked Liddy on her hind legs, dressed in all of her finery with the plume waving on her bonnet. Behind her came Grushenka, pushing a baby carriage. In the carriage lay Tip with a baby's cap tied over his ears and a bottle in his mouth. This was the part of the show that Tip liked best, because the professor always saw to it that there was real milk in the bottle.

Now around the side of the house came Sancho, walking on his hind legs and dressed in his scarlet jacket and yellow trousers. He bowed politely to Liddy, waving his beautiful tail. Liddy bowed to Sancho. Together they began to waltz.

By this time Prince had been hurried into his orange and green outfit, and he also came walking on his hind legs around the house. The professor was playing his jaw harp, and Prince and Grushenka were soon waltzing beside the others. It was a pretty sight. Even Tip, having finished the milk in his bottle, leaped out of the baby carriage and began to waltz to the great delight of the children. When he had waltzed a few measures, Tip went down on all fours and approached the audience. In a moment he had extracted a large gold watch and chain from the pocket of an old gentleman who was watching the dancers.

Poor Professor Petit was obliged to stop playing the jaw harp and return the watch to the gentleman, who had not even missed it. Whether or not this was a regular part of the show, Willie could not tell, but it is certain that the audience was greatly amused.

Amid the applause Willie heard only one discordant note. Behind him there was a low sound of growling, and a man's voice said, "Not yet, Brutus! Wait a little longer."

*I should warn Professor Petit*, Willie thought. *I believe that Hoskins and Brutus are up to no good.*

But there seemed no way to get a message to the professor, for, once his show had begun, it moved steadily forward with the precision of a clock. Now Liddy was performing her act on the ladder and tightrope, and Grushenka was balancing a ball on her nose and tossing it into the air. Willie could see that the pony was hitched to the red fire cart, and was standing by in readiness for the next act. Professor Petit seemed to be everywhere at once: now setting up ladders, now tossing Grushenka a ball, now slipping the red harness over the pony's head. And now he was behind the little house lighting a paper flare.

In an instant the whole scene changed. Fire and smoke began to come out of the chimney of the house, and Tip in his baby's cap appeared at an upper window as if he wished to be saved. Grushenka left her ball and ran to pull the cord of a fire bell with her mouth.

Professor Petit cried out in a strong voice: "Fetch water! Fetch ladder! Fire! Fire!"

Prince and Sancho, with buckets dangling from

their mouths, ran to the river for water. The pony pranced onto the scene, drawing the red cart. Liddy and Grushenka hopped onto the cart as it stopped before the little house. Together they took hold of the ladder on the cart and set it up against the house. Then Liddy, with the nozzle of a hose in her mouth, began slowly to climb the ladder. In the meantime Prince and Sancho returned from the river, spilling the contents of their buckets into a small tank on the red cart. As they dashed back to the river for more water, Grushenka began to bob up and down with her paws on the handle of a pump. The pump sent water up into the hose. Liddy held the nozzle pointed toward the house, and in a moment water was squirting out of the hose onto the fire. There was a hiss and a crackle, a crackle and a hiss, as fire and water met.

The children shrieked with pleasure and excitement as they saw the highly trained dogs putting out the fire. Nothing more wonderful than this had ever been seen in Puddling Center. Willie cried out also, and clapped his hands together until they stung. But in the midst of his delight, some impulse made him turn to look at the large man and his dog. And he was just in time to see Hulk Hoskins stooping to unfasten Brutus's leash. He saw the flash of white teeth in the snarling face of the dog, and he heard the man's muttered, *"Go!"*

# DOG FIGHT

The big dog named Brutus went like a flash. Before Willie could cry out to warn Professor Petit, Brutus had leapt in among the actors, biting and snapping. The fire was out, and Liddy and Tip were descending the ladder from the window of the house. Grushenka was still busy at the pump, and Prince and Sancho were returning from the river. They were all in their costumes and unprepared for attack.

When the strange dog leapt among them, the pony became frightened and began to run. The ladder fell down with Liddy and Tip tumbling off it in midair. Grushenka jumped from the cart and made for Brutus, but she was no match for his great strength. The other highly trained dogs rushed to her assistance from all sides. They were down on all fours now, and as full of fight as if they had never been educated for better things. But, although they were five against one, Brutus had all of the advantage. He had not been taken by surprise, nor was he hampered by trousers and petticoats. His wide, strong collar, on which his name was spelled, only made it more difficult for the highly trained dogs to catch him by the throat.

The children and Miss Charmian began to scream and cry out. The barking and snarling of the dogs was terrific. Professor Petit ran out shouting commands, but he was scarcely heard over the uproar. This was one time when he might have used a whip to good advantage. But he did not even own one, for he had never before needed it.

"Stop this! Stop this!" he cried. But, when his dogs tried to obey him, they were ever more savagely set upon by the strange dog. Willie stood up and shouted, too. At first he shouted "Stop!", and then he quite forgot himself and began to shout, "Sic 'em! Go it! Eat the big brute alive!"

It was a terrible fight. In the midst of it all, Willie suddenly remembered Brutus's master. He turned around to beg Hulk Hoskins, in the name of common decency, to call off his dog. But the large stranger was no longer there. He had unleashed Brutus and gone away. Let the highly trained dogs look after themselves!

Now Willie remembered the fire hose. The pony

had run a little way, and then had stopped and begun to eat daisies and buttercups. It took Willie only a moment to back the cart, man the pump, and point the nozzle at Brutus's nose. There was not very much water left in the tank, but a thin stream directed in Brutus's face was enough to turn the tide of battle.

Brutus spluttered and gasped with surprise. He stopped fighting to shake himself, and instantly the five highly trained dogs pounced on him. As soon as he saw that the fight was going against him, Brutus began to run. At a word from Professor Petit, the highly trained dogs let him go—all except Tip, who hung on to his tail all the way across the square.

Finally, however, Brutus broke away and, running swiftly, disappeared out of town. The highly trained dogs chased him a short distance, and then they came limping back to their master. They were a sorry sight. Trousers and jackets were torn, ears were bloody, legs were lame. The beautiful little house had been knocked over, so that everyone could see it was not a real house, after all, but only a show house. It was apparent that the performance was over for that day.

To make matters worse, the people of Puddling Center, even the children, began to come up now and ask for their money back.

"We expected a good performance," they said.

"We did not get our money's worth."

Willie tried to reason with them, and tell them that perhaps the show could be repeated later when the dogs had had a rest. He told them that they were really lucky to have seen more than they had bargained for.

But Professor Petit said, "Give them back their money, Willie. We are honest showmen, and we have been prevented from completing an honest show. We cannot, with good conscience, keep a penny."

So, reluctantly, Willie handed back the people's shillings until the money bag was empty.

When he returned to the green caravan, he found that Professor Petit was busy dressing the wounds and making the dogs comfortable.

"What is to be done now, Professor?" Willie asked.

"Alas!" said Professor Petit. "Now, indeed, we are ruined. I shall have to stop here and get some sort of employment to keep us alive, while I mend the costumes, repair the little house, and gather fresh courage to go on."

"Did you recognize the dog that caused the trouble?" Willie asked. "I'm sure I know who it was."

"Yes," said the professor. "It was Brutus from Hulk Hoskins's show."

"His master was here, too," said Willie. "I saw him

unleash Brutus, and then he went away."

"It is a cruel thing to have an enemy," said the professor. "I did not think that I should ever have one, and, indeed, I have done nothing to deserve such treatment from Hulk Hoskins. It is only our skill and excellence that has made him jealous. He wants us entirely out of his way."

"I notice that you put the blame on the master and not on the dog," said Willie.

"Yes," said Professor Petit. "The dog is not to be blamed, for a dog will always reflect the character of his master. If you find an ugly, snarling dog, mark my words, you will soon discover that he belongs to a cross and cruel master."

Willie noticed that, in spite of their bandages and patches, Professor Petit's dogs were still wagging their tails and regarding their master with hope and kindness. *It is easy to see*, he thought to himself, *that these dogs have a good master.*

"How would you advise me to try and earn my living, Willie?" asked the professor. "I could teach singing and dancing to the people of Puddling Center. Do you think they would like that?"

Willie thought of Uncle Scrivens and the other serious people of Puddling Center.

"I'm afraid not," Willie said. "The people here do

not have time for singing and dancing. They believe that it is more important to be rich than to enjoy themselves."

"Ah!" said Professor Petit.

"But I'll tell you what," said Willie. "If you were willing to let your dogs work for you, I am sure that they could get regular employment with the miller, the weaver, the farmer, and the baker. I'd be glad to have them earn the money that I have been receiving in that way; and then perhaps I could find a little time to go to school."

The dogs began to bark, as if they had perfectly understood Willie's proposal. They jumped up and put their paws against the professor's legs. Liddy sat up and begged. Only Tip went into a corner and rolled himself up in a ball and fell asleep.

"Well, bless my soul!" said Professor Petit. "What is the meaning of all this?"

"They had a good time this morning," Willie said. "I believe that it would be a kind of vacation for them to work in Puddling Center for a little while instead of giving shows."

So it came about that Prince went to work for the baker, Sancho for the farmer, Grushenka for the weaver, and Liddy for the miller.

"And what shall Tip do?" Willie asked.

"Tip shall go to school with you," said the professor. "That is, if Miss Charmian will have him. He is very ignorant, and perhaps he will learn something in school that I have been unable to teach him. Meantime I shall occupy myself with mending and repairing and thinking up some new acts for the show. I am far from beaten, as Hulk Hoskins himself will one day find out."

The next day, when Willie had delivered Uncle Scrivens's letters and was ready to go to school, the professor handed him a note for Miss Charmian, and Tip trotted along beside him.

*Dear Miss Charmian,* said the note. *I hope that you will not mind having a dog in school. The rest of my dogs are highly educated, but Tip has set his mind against learning. I trust that you can help him.*

*Respectfully yours,*
*Pierre Petit.*

# TIP GOES TO SCHOOL

Tip sat beside Willie, while the teacher read the note, and he wagged his tail in such a friendly way that she did not have the heart to say no.

The little children were all tittering and laughing behind their geographies to see a dog in school. This was most unusual, because the children of Puddling Center were ordinarily as solemn as their parents. Miss Charmian rapped on her desk and said, "Quiet, please."

When everything was quiet, she said, "How many of you are glad to see Willie back in school?"

All of the children raised their hands.

"He has brought another pupil with him," continued Miss Charmian, "who is in need of instruction. The new pupil is named Tip."

At the sound of his name Tip lay down on the floor and rolled over, so quickly that in an instant he was up again and looking as solemn as a judge. The children had to cover their mouths with their hands to keep from laughing.

"Now," said Miss Charmian, "we can only allow Tip to stay, if he will behave *him*self, and if you children will behave *your*selves, and if Willie sees to it that there is no disturbance."

"Yes, ma'am," Willie said. He went and sat down in the one large seat at the back of the schoolroom and motioned to Tip to sit beside him.

"Now," said Miss Charmian, "let us continue with our geography lesson. Lucy Tufts, will you kindly bound Nigeria?"

Willie opened the geography to Nigeria, and followed with his finger the boundaries of the country as Lucy recited them. He felt very happy to be here and to be learning something new and interesting. In a few moments he was sure that he could close the book and bound Nigeria also, if Miss Charmian were to ask him.

For a while Tip sat up quite straight beside Willie, listening carefully to all that was said. But presently he began to yawn and his tail to droop. Very slowly he sank down, curled himself into a ball, and went to sleep.

Willie thought that school was not going to do Tip very much good, but, if only he behaved himself, it would surely do him no harm.

Recess, however, was quite a different matter. Tip woke up with a start, as the children marched out of the schoolroom, and he went racing between their legs to be the first one out of doors. As usual the children made a neat ring to play Drop the Handkerchief. But the very first time the handkerchief was dropped, Tip made off with it, and dashed away across the school yard. In a moment all of the children were after him, laughing and shouting in a most unusual way. Tip leaped over the swing boards and ran under the teeter-totter with all of the children tearing after him. Eventually it turned into a wonderful game of tag. "Tip-Tag," the children called it. They had never been so red-cheeked and out of breath and full of laughter in their lives as they were when they came in from recess.

After recess they had singing, and usually the children sang in very gentle little birdlike voices. But today they shouted at the tops of their lungs, and Tip sang, too, "Ow-wow-wow-wow-wow!" Miss Charmian did not know whether to be pleased or not, but she was impressed. There was no naughtiness at all, only a great deal of enthusiasm and good cheer.

When school was out Willie and Tip returned to the green caravan, and found that the other dogs were there, too, each having done his work satisfactorily.

"I wish they could tell us their experiences,"

Professor Petit said. "It is such a pity that they cannot *speak*!"

"How are you, my friend?" said Sancho when he heard the word *speak*.

"Good Sancho!" cried the professor, laying a kindly hand on Sancho's head. "You would tell us, if you could, how you have spent your day, wouldn't you, my friend?" The dogs all barked and wagged their tails when they heard the question in his voice.

Beyond the trees at the other corner of the public square, Willie could see that something unusual was taking place.

"What is going on there?" he asked. "Is someone putting up a tent?"

"Yes," said the professor gloomily. "Hoskins's Circus has arrived in town. Hulk Hoskins is putting up his tent. Tomorrow he will show his tiger."

Hulk Hoskins traveled in a much larger caravan than Professor Petit's. It was pulled by two horses. Mr. Hoskins also had two assistants, who were as unpleasant looking as himself. Out of the caravan the three men took a large, striped tent which they began to put up on the corner of the square nearest the post office.

All of the people of Puddling Center came out to watch the tent go up. Two shows in town at once!

It had been a long time since they had seen so much excitement.

But Hulk Hoskins put a rope fence all around his tent, so that the people could not get too close or look inside it. If any of them tried to creep under the rope, the big gray dog, Brutus, snarled at them, so that they quickly crept back again. But even at a distance they could see the black bear that was led out of the caravan and into the tent. They could see two sad-looking monkeys that hopped along at the ends of a chain.

"Where is the tiger?" everybody asked Hulk Hoskins, but he would not bother to answer them.

"Be sensible," Uncle Scrivens said to the people. "If he showed you the tiger now, you would not pay your money and go to the show. This Hoskins is a smart man. Someday I expect he will be rich."

"Ah, yes," the people said. "A smart man who will be very rich."

They tried to peer inside the caravan, but it was dark inside and they could see nothing. Every so often, however, they could hear the tiger roar. The roar began with a kind of whirring and rasping noise, and then it would grow louder and become a great roar, and then it would fade away gradually, as if the tiger's voice had run down, and then there would be silence.

"Ah! the tiger is roaring!" the people said. "Listen

to it! Isn't it terrible?"

Willie also listened when the tiger roared. He had never heard a tiger roar before, but the sound was not exactly what he had expected. "The tiger's roar is something like the sound of a foghorn or a mechanical saw," he said to himself. "Yes, it is very terrible, but not quite as I thought it would be." He was more eager than ever to see the tiger.

"Will it hurt your feelings, Professor Petit, if I go to see Hulk Hoskins's show?" he asked.

"No, my boy," said the professor quietly. "Go, by all means. But keep your eyes open for anything that happens. And especially notice if there is skill and kindness in the show. Skill and kindness should be in every good show, as well as joy and art."

While the people of Puddling Center were in bed that night, Hulk Hoskins and his assistants must have moved the tiger from the caravan into the tent. For in the morning the sound of roaring, which occurred at intervals of ten or fifteen minutes, came from the tent instead of from the caravan.

"I hope he is in a good strong cage," people said. "A tiger's claws would make short work of a canvas tent!" They were frightened as well as thrilled, and they went about their work more solemnly than ever. Only the children of Puddling Center were happy that day, but that, of course, was because they had Tip in school.

The rest of Professor Petit's Highly Trained Dogs went about their work as usual: Sancho to herd the farmer's sheep, Prince to pull the baker's cart, Grushenka to help the weaver, and Liddy to catch the miller's rats.

"Aren't you afraid that Brutus will bother them, Professor?" Willie asked.

"I truly hope not," said Professor Petit. "Brutus will be busy guarding the tent and performing in his master's show today. Last night he was on the prowl, but I saw to it that my own dogs were safely enclosed in my caravan during the night so that they were not in his way."

"How do you know he was out?"

"I heard him sniffing about our wagon, looking for stray bones. Hulk Hoskins's animals are only half fed and must fend for themselves, so I have heard."

"I hope this is not true of the tiger," Willie said anxiously.

"Probably not," said Professor Petit. "The tiger is Mr. Hoskins's greatest attraction, and I have no doubt that he is better fed than all the other animals."

At school that day, Willie learned to multiply by nine, to tell the difference between an isthmus and a peninsula, and to spell Constantinople. If Tip learned anything it would be difficult to say. But at recess he taught the children a new game which was something like leapfrog in a sort of over-and-under way and was called "Tip-Top."

After recess the children returned red-cheeked and breathless to their seats. Tip was the last one to come in, and he carried in his mouth a large red apple, which he deposited at Miss Charmian's feet. The children roared with laughter, all except Willie, who was very much afraid that someone would be missing a large red apple from his dinner pail at noon.

Miss Charmian flushed, and, putting the apple on her desk, she rapped three times for order. Tip trotted quietly back to his place beside Willie, but it took the children several minutes to settle down. When she could be heard, Miss Charmian said, "Children! Children! Please remember your manners. I don't know what has come over you! And I was just about to tell you that if you work unusually well this afternoon, you will be excused a half an hour early to attend Hoskins's Circus."

Instead of folding their hands and smiling politely, the children bounced in their seats and shouted, *"Hooray!"* But then they saw that Tip was sitting up quietly looking at Miss Charmian with great attention, so they all became quiet, too, and studied as hard as they could.

# HOSKINS'S CIRCUS

At half past two a great crowd of people had assembled in front of Hoskins's striped tent. Every fifteen minutes or oftener the tiger could be heard roaring. Besides this there was a sound of music. One of Hoskins's assistants turned the handle of a barrel organ which ground out a mechanical tune. No one in Hoskins's Circus knew how to play the jaw harp as Professor Petit did, but the barrel organ, if not so artful, was at least much louder.

The children marched down from school two by two. But instead of walking, they skipped most of the way because Tip was skipping. Willie skipped beside Miss Charmian.

"Have you ever seen a tiger?" he asked Miss Charmian.

"No," she replied. "I'm just as excited as you are."

Besides the shilling price of admission there was a penny tax. "To pay for the oil on the flaming hoop," explained the assistant who sold the tickets.

"Ah, yes," the people said, feeling in their pockets for the extra pennies.

Willie looked across the square at Professor Petit's green caravan, but it was closed and silent. Professor Petit was evidently inside, and the dogs had not returned from their work.

Nobody thought to pay Tip's way into Hoskins's Circus, but he went sniffing and poking about the outside of the tent, until one of the assistants drove him away. When he went, he carried a loose tent peg in his mouth, and he lay down under the green caravan to chew it up before he went to sleep.

Inside the striped tent there were rows of plank seats and a stage with red curtains hanging at the back. It was more like a theatre than a circus, Willie thought, although he could see straps and swings for some sort of aerial performance. There was a hanging lamp that made the inside of the tent as light as day.

When the seats were filled, the red curtains parted and Hoskins himself stepped onto the stage. He was dressed very splendidly in a black uniform decorated with medals and shining gold braid. In his hand he carried a large black whip, which he cracked with a wonderful noise like the report of a gun.

"Ladies and gentlemen," he said. "Welcome to Hoskins's Cir—" As he was speaking the tiger began to roar. Inside the tent the sound was almost deafening. The audience could not see the tiger because he was behind the red curtain, but everyone knew that he was very near. A chill went up and down Willie's spine as he thought how near the tiger was. While the roaring continued, Hulk Hoskins stood still and waited. He looked at the audience and smiled. The light from the lamp shone on his white teeth and on the gold hoops in his ears. It shone on his medals and his gold braid. His very eyes glittered and shone with pride and triumph, and all this while the tiger roared.

When his voice could be heard again, Hulk Hoskins went on with his speech of welcome. The speech was full of long words and flowery phrases, and Willie thought, *If Professor Petit were giving this show, he would not talk about his acts, but he would let us see them.*

At last, however, Hoskins's Circus began. With much cracking of the whip, the bear was led out at the end of a chain and made to dance. Next the two monkeys were led out and made to swing and leap about on the overhead trapeze. One of them was also able to ride a little velocipede around and around the stage. The monkey looked very sad as he rode. His small red eyes, set close together, blinked as if they were full of tears. But the people of Puddling Center were pleased and clapped their hands. "Perhaps it is because they are all so serious in Puddling Center," Willie thought. "They do not know a happy act from a sad one. They do not see that Professor Petit's animals are happy, whilst these animals are low-spirited and sad."

Next Brutus came out upon the stage, and grasped the end of a leather strap in his teeth. While the barrel organ played a polka, one of the assistants began to turn a handle which wound a rope over a pulley and around a winch. Holding on by his teeth, Brutus was gradually raised to the very top of the tent.

*Crack!* went the whip. *Toodle-doodle-do!* went the barrel organ.

"Ah-h-h!" said the people of Puddling Center, and Uncle Scrivens, who had a good front seat, nodded his head and said: "A modern show, a mechanical show! None of your old-fashioned foolishness here. This works like clockwork. It will make Mr. Hoskins rich!"

The whip cracked again, and Brutus was slowly lowered to the stage. Willie could see the strength of his jaw and how his neck swelled under the brass-studded collar. Even Willie had to admire Brutus's strength.

"And now, ladies and gentlemen!" cried Mr. Hoskins, "we are come to the supreme and super-stupendous pinnacle of our show. We are about to show you our tiger performing his magnificent and supercolossal feat of leaping through a flaming hoop." At this moment the tiger roared again, and everyone had to wait until he was through roaring before they could hear what Hulk Hoskins said.

The children clutched each other in pleasurable terror, and even Miss Charmian took hold of Willie's arm as if the two of them together could bear the sight of the tiger more easily than either one alone.

The barrel organ began to grind out a loud and exciting tune. Slowly the red curtains parted. Hulk Hoskins stepped back and picked up a hoop which had been wound in oil-soaked paper. One of the assistants took a long spill of twisted paper and lighted it at the lamp. He carried it to the stage and applied it to the hoop. The fire began to race around the hoop so that the whole thing soon burned very brightly. Hoskins cracked his whip. There was a loud whirring sound and another roar. A large orange-and-black striped body leapt from behind one red curtain, through the flaming hoop, and away behind the other red curtain, so quickly that the audience was left gasping.

"The tiger!" they said. "We have seen the tiger!" They began to applaud very loudly. "More! More!" they cried. "We want to see it again."

But by now the flaming hoop had gone out and the show was over.

In spite of having seen such an exciting thing, people somehow felt a little disappointed. Their hopes had been high, and the tiger's appearance had been very brief.

"Come again tomorrow, my friends," said Hoskins, smiling his shiny smile, "if you would like to see more of the tiger."

Uncle Scrivens nodded his head in approval. "Hoskins is a smart man," he said. "He knows that familiarity breeds contempt. If we had seen all we wished of the tiger, we would not come back for another performance."

Willie went away, wondering, but he, too, wanted to return the next day for a better view of the tiger.

"I will go and talk with Professor Petit," he said to himself.

# EVENING CAMPFIRE

Professor Petit was sitting by a campfire between his caravan and the river. The highly trained dogs were all assembled about him cheerfully, expecting their supper. Liddy and Tip were chasing each other and barking. Grushenka was playing with a ball. Prince was sitting up quietly, gazing into the fire, and Sancho lay beside his master sleeping, with his head resting on his paws. Sancho's beautiful black coat was stained and dirty. His paws were covered with mud.

"Sancho must have had a hard day," said Professor Petit. "He is tired and dirty. It is too bad that such a highly trained dog should have to herd sheep and cows. Yet I am very thankful for the wages my dogs are earning. I have been repairing and making new costumes, and tonight we have a banquet fit for a king."

He lifted the lid of the cooking pot, and Willie

could smell a wonderful odor of bubbling meat and vegetables. "And plenty of bones to go around after the stew is lapped up, too," added the professor. "Of course you will dine with us, Willie, my boy?"

"Thank you," said Willie, "I'd admire to do so."

"And so you saw Hoskins's show, Willie? Tell me frankly what you thought of it. If it is really very good I shall be glad to know it. You see, I had rather be beaten by a very *good* show than by a poor one."

"Well," said Willie, "people seemed to enjoy the show. But I looked for the things you told me, and I did not think that it was very skillful or kind or happy. But perhaps I was not in the proper frame of mind."

"And the tiger?" asked the professor. "Did you see the tiger?"

"Yes," Willie said, "but only for an instant as he dashed through the hoop. I would like to have a chance to see him more clearly. Mr. Hoskins wants everybody to come back tomorrow to look at the tiger again."

"Ah," said the professor. He stirred the stew with a long wooden spoon. He seemed to be thinking. Liddy and Tip came and sat beside the fire with their tongues hanging out and their tails wagging. They fixed their eyes on the pot of food and lifted up their noses to sniff.

"Hoskins is a clever showman," continued the professor. "An honest showman would let you gaze your fill at his show, but Hoskins wants you to go away unsatisfied, so that you will return and buy another ticket. But I had hoped to hear more about the tiger than this from you, Willie. There is something strange about this tiger of Hoskins's."

"What do you mean?" asked Willie.

"Well," said the professor, "you see how my dogs make use of their noses?" He pointed to Liddy and Tip, and Willie laughed.

"They think your stew smells like supper," he said.

"Dogs have a much keener sense of smell than human beings have, as you know. No matter if I had washed myself thoroughly and put on a strange suit of clothing, my dogs would recognize me by my own personal odor which I do not even recognize myself. If you were to come knocking on the caravan door in the dark of night, my dogs would sniff your odor and wag their tails because they know now that you are their friend."

"But what does this have to do with the tiger?" Willie asked.

"Just this," said Professor Petit, "that tame animals, such as dogs and horses, are very sensitive to the odors of wild animals. Even the roan pony will not go near a tent of wild animals if he can help it, and in the past, whenever we have been near a display of lions, tigers, or other wild beasts, the dogs have been in a continual uproar of barking and growling."

"But tonight they are perfectly calm," said Willie.

"Exactly," said Professor Petit. "That is why I am puzzled. They sniffed and barked a little at Hoskins's bear, but it is a poor, sad animal, born in captivity and long domesticated. The tiger, roaring as it does so fearfully, is quite a different matter. With so much ferocious sound, the tiger should have a ferocious scent. Yet my dogs have not detected it. This seems strange to me. Ah, well, it is time for supper."

At the word *supper*, all of the dogs were on their feet, except Sancho. He opened his eyes and looked around, stretching his legs and yawning so that his red tongue curled up in his mouth. He seemed more tired than hungry.

"Now, friends," said the professor, "don't crowd. The stew would burn your mouths at present. It's got to cool, children, it's got to cool."

"Sancho is always wise," said Willie. "He understands that there is no use in hurrying."

"Sancho is very tired," said Professor Petit. "If I did not know that he dislikes fighting, I would say he had blood on his coat. But such an idea is really absurd. He has probably had to chase after a stray sheep, and perhaps got into a bog or a swamp."

At mention of his name, Sancho rose slowly and came to stand with the other dogs beside the pan of stew that was cooling for them. Willie bent to examine his coat. "He has certainly got a lot of burs in it," he said. "After supper we will have to give him a good brushing."

"Each dog is beginning to wear the marks of his trade," said the professor. "Liddy and Prince have flour on their coats from mill and bakery; Grushenka has lint from the weaver's loom sticking to her back; and Tip's black spots are marked with chalk. It is no wonder that Sancho looks like a sheep herder."

Professor Petit was a good cook, and Willie found the dinner very tasty.

"You cook for your dogs," he said, "as if they were kings."

"My dear Willie," replied the professor, "whatever a person does, he should do as well as he can. The greatest pleasure in life really, is in giving a good performance, whether it be an exhibit of skill before a distinguished audience or only a stew which one expects to share with his dog. Remember that, please. It is quite important."

"Very well, Professor. I will try to remember."

When they had finished eating and the dogs were

lying, each one by itself, gnawing a bone, there came a rustle beyond the fire. It had grown dark now, and, looking up, Willie saw two eyes, like balls of fire, glowing with the reflection of the flame. At once the dogs began to growl, the hair along their backs rising in little ridges of anger. Willie thought of the tiger, but then he heard the professor saying to his dogs, "Be still, friends. It's only Brutus, and you're a match for him when your jackets are off."

Professor Petit went to the cooling stew kettle and pulled out a bone, which he threw across the fire to the big gray dog.

"My poor Brutus," he said, "you are hungry. We can do no less than be kind."

Brutus seized the bone and ran away with it in the darkness. All of the highly trained dogs, except Sancho, returned to their own bones in peaceful quiet. But, for a long time, Sancho continued to growl. His eyes gleamed in the firelight, and his lips drew back from his white teeth in a snarl of disgust.

"It is better to forgive and forget, my good dog," said the professor. "It is only the elephant who remembers his grievances long beyond their natural term."

Sancho rose stiffly and came to his master's side. He laid his head on Professor Petit's knee, as if he would like to tell him something.

# SANCHO IN TROUBLE

As Willie was going to school the next day, he met Farmer Olney driving into town in his two-wheeled cart.

"Don't go to school today, Willie," the farmer called, "because I shall need you to herd my cattle and sheep."

"But what about Sancho?" Willie cried. "Isn't he better than I am at herding sheep?"

"Alas!" said the farmer. "The fool I am to trust a dog alone with my sheep! Your fine little dog has killed two sheep and run the others nearly to death. I'll have no more dogs for sheep herders, thank you!"

Willie came up beside the cart with Tip at his heels. "Oh, I can't believe that Sancho would kill your sheep, sir!" he cried. "There's some mistake, I'm sure."

"Mistake, indeed!" said the farmer. "Do you think I

am mistaken when I find two of my sheep lying dead in the pasture, with their throats bitten through? Half of their blood has been sucked by that miserable dog, and the rest is spilled on the sandy ground. As for the other sheep, their wool is full of burs, and they are tired out as if they had been run all over the pasture in wicked sport. I'll tell you, your highly trained dog has been amusing himself very cruelly at my expense, Willie."

"But, dear me!" Willie cried. "Sancho is the wisest and best of all the professor's dogs."

"Aye, he is wise enough," said Farmer Olney, "but he's also the sliest and the most wicked. Such a dog must not be allowed to live to go on killing sheep. As for the master, he must pay me well for the sheep I have lost or I'll have him thrown into jail."

"Poor Professor Petit!" said Willie. "Here's more trouble for him!"

"Climb in," said the farmer, "if you care to come along and see what happens."

Willie climbed up into the farmer's cart, and Tip was about to follow, but the farmer cried, "Be off with you! I'll have no more to do with these highly trained dogs!"

"Tip," said Willie, "go on to school, like a good boy. I'll come as soon as I can."

Tip sat down beside the road and watched the

cart out of sight. His tail with the black tip drooped, and his ears hung down very sadly. But after a time he got up and shook himself, and started away in the direction of the school. It was hard for him to be sad very long, and presently his tail was waving again and he was stopping along the way to explore all the gopher holes, and sniff the delightful morning smells. When he arrived at school he was carrying in his mouth a long, pointed stick which Miss Charmian found very useful as a blackboard pointer.

"But when did this terrible thing occur?" asked Professor Petit. Willie could see that the professor was deeply troubled and confused.

"How should I be able to say *when*?" cried Mr. Olney angrily. "It is not a matter of *when* but *what*. All I know is that your fine dog did not bring all of my sheep home last night. At first I didn't see that two were missing. Then later, when I made the count and went into the fields to hunt, I found my two good sheep lying dead in their blood. What am I to suppose? Why, it's plain as the nose on your face that this dog of yours has killed them for his sport."

"I can't believe it," Professor Petit said sadly. He shook his head, repeating, "I cannot believe it!"

Willie noticed that all of the dogs, except Sancho, had gone to their daily work. Sancho still sat by the ashes of the breakfast fire, his tail drooping and his dark eyes sad.

"Look at him!" cried the farmer. "Guilt is written all over him! A hang-dog look, if ever I saw one. He must be put out of the way before he does any more damage."

"No!" cried the professor. "He has been in some kind of trouble, I'll admit. But I'm sure he is innocent of any evil. If only he could tell us! If only he could *speak*!"

"How are you, my friend?" said Sancho in a dejected voice.

Farmer Olney nearly jumped out of his skin. But the very next moment he was angrier than ever.

"The devil's in him!" he cried. "Who ever heard an honest dog use words? It's wicked and unnatural! He must be killed at once."

By this time a small crowd had begun to assemble.

"It's unnatural! It's wicked!" the townspeople said. "The dog must be killed."

"I've sent for the policeman," said Mr. Olney. "But first, Professor, I'll give you the opportunity of paying me ten dollars apiece for my two dead sheep and another five dollars for the mental anguish I have suffered."

"Twenty-five dollars!" Professor Petit said. "Then

you must give me a little time, Mr. Olney. For where in the world can I find so much money all at once?"

"No," said the farmer, "I'll give you no time. You are a traveling showman and all you need do is pack up your caravan and drive away to be rid of your debts. You must pay me today or go to jail."

In vain Professor Petit and Willie tried to explain that an honest showman would always pay his honest debts. Farmer Olney was not a bad man, but, like all of the serious people of Puddling Center, he believed that where money was concerned, no one could be trusted.

The upshot of it all was that the Puddling Center policeman arrived and agreed to take Professor Petit and his dog to jail until they could be tried and sentenced.

"Well, take me if you *must*," Professor Petit said. "But leave my poor dog free. Jail is no place for a dog."

"What! Leave that dog free to roam the countryside and kill more sheep!" cried the farmer. "Why, he's the very one we want in jail. The dog must be killed, I say."

Willie followed along with the crowd as the professor and his highly trained dog were led away to prison. The boy's heart was sad, for he felt that the showman and his dogs were the best friends he had in this very serious town. And he could not bear to think of Sancho losing his life.

At the door of the prison Professor Petit turned to Willie and held out his hand. There were tears in his eyes, and his brisk and cheerful manner had deserted him.

"Willie," he said, "I beg you to look after the four remaining dogs and the pony whilst I am away. They will not understand what has happened and you must comfort them."

"I'll be proud to do everything I can," Willie said, "and you must not worry."

"Of course," said the professor, "I could sell the caravan or the pony or one of the dogs to raise the money, but that would break my heart. But the first thing is to prove my poor dog's innocence. How I shall do it, I do not know. Help me if you can, Willie! Help me!"

"Hurry up now," said the policeman. "In you go, and no more palavering!"

"I will try, Professor," Willie called, as the heavy door of jail closed behind master and dog.

Little sunny towns very seldom have prisons. But Puddling Center was a serious town, and it had built a large and serious prison. As a matter of fact, the cells were usually unoccupied; so now the jailer, the policeman, and the serious citizens were delighted to find someone to lock up at last. They put Professor

Petit and Sancho in a small room with a barred window high up in the prison.

"He is so high up that he cannot be reached by his friends," said the jailer. "The only way he could get out would be to saw through the iron bars and let himself down by two or three bedsheets knotted together. But, as he has neither saw nor bedsheets, I believe that he will be quite safe."

# HOSKINS MAKES
# AN OFFER

Willie went back to the caravan, and tethered the roan pony in a fresh spot where there was plenty of clover to eat. He washed the pots and pans at the edge of the river, and then he tidied the inside of the caravan. All of the time he kept thinking to himself: *What next? Without Professor Petit's wise counsel, how shall I know what is best to do? Shall I try to give shows to raise money? But the dogs would probably not go through their tricks for* me, *and anyhow who would come to see them with Hoskins's tiger in town? It's all very difficult.*

When the dogs came home from work, they ran all around the caravan sniffing and searching for their master. Willie had built up the fire and put on a kettle of bones to simmer.

"Come, friends," he said to the dogs, "your master

is in trouble, and we must help him, but I don't know how to make you understand."

The three working dogs, with Tip, who had just arrived from school, came and stood around Willie, wagging their tails and gazing expectantly into his face. Willie could see that they wanted very much to be helpful and agreeable, but that they did not understand what was required of them. *It is hard to be a dog*, Willie thought. *A dog is full of love and goodwill, but he does not have a language!*

As if they had read his mind, the dogs all began to bark at him.

"Yes, yes," said Willie, laughing, "you do have a language of your own, don't you? And probably you are sorry for *me* because I can't understand you. Sancho is the only one who understands a little of both languages. But *Sancho* is not here."

At the sound of Sancho's name, Prince ran to the caravan and came dragging out the box that contained Sancho's alphabet. He pulled the box in front of Willie, and then he stepped back and barked as if he expected Willie to produce Sancho.

Sadly Willie put the box away again, and gave the dogs their supper.

As they were eating, Willie heard a familiar growl, and he saw the hair rising along the backs of

Professor Petit's dogs. Looking around, he saw that Hulk Hoskins and Brutus were coming across the square toward them. Hoskins had Brutus on a leash, but Willie knew how easily the leash could be slipped off, and he began to be alarmed.

*I must not let the dogs see that I am frightened*, he thought, and to the dogs he said, "Steady now, friends. Don't fight, unless he starts it."

The dogs stood at attention, stiff-legged and alert, sniffing the air and ready for anything. But Hulk Hoskins appeared to be in a friendly mood tonight. His teeth flashed in a wide white smile.

"I hear that Professor Petit and one of his dogs have gone to prison for their evil deeds," said Hulk Hoskins in a winning voice. He jingled the money in his pocket, and Willie knew that he must have a great deal of it, for the performance that afternoon had been as well attended as the one on the previous day. "I am sorry for Professor Petit," continued Mr. Hoskins, "but what can a sinful man expect? The law is bound to catch up with him sooner or later."

"But Professor Petit is not a sinful man," cried Willie. "He's one of the best I've ever known."

"Ah, well," said Mr. Hoskins, still smiling very broadly. "Then let us say that he has trained a sinful dog. But, as I say, I'm sorry for him. I understand that he needs money to pay for the damage his dog has done. Now I am willing to take over his caravan, his pony, and the four dogs that remain after the sinful one has been executed. I will add them, unimportant as they are, to my stupendous and colossal show, and at the same time I will be so generous and kind-hearted as to settle Professor Petit's debts for him and get him out of prison. Thus, he can start out once again, a free man, and, we hope, a more honest one."

"You mean—?" cried Willie. "You mean to say—?"

"Exactly," said Hulk Hoskins. His white teeth still flashed, but Willie had the impression of a snarl rather than a smile. "I will buy Professor Petit's show for the price of his debts. What could be fairer?"

"Oh, no!" said Willie. "There must be some better way than that. His debts are only twenty-five dollars, and his highly trained dogs are worth a great deal more than that."

"But who will pay it?" asked Hulk Hoskins. "Who would have any use for a show except another showman? Have you thought of that?"

"Oh," said Willie, "I'm sure he could sell Prince to the baker, Liddy to the miller, and Grushenka to the weaver, if the worst came to the worst."

"And separate them?" said Hulk Hoskins. "Wouldn't that be a pity now?"

"Yes, it would," said Willie. "But we still have one hope."

"And what is that?"

"That we may prove Sancho innocent."

"Ha! Ha!" laughed Hulk Hoskins. "Pardon me, if I seem to laugh."

As they were talking, Willie noticed that Brutus had settled down beside his master and was trying to remove a bur from his back just above his tail. He twisted this way and that, but he could not quite reach the bur, either with his teeth or with his hind paws.

"Well," said Mr. Hoskins, "there is my offer, made out of the kindness of my heart, for the good of all concerned. Think it over and let me know. Come along, Brutus."

But Brutus was intent on his bur and paid no attention until Hulk Hoskins roared at him and struck him with the end of the leash.

"That will teach you!" the showman cried. "Come along now!"

Brutus jumped up with a yelp and followed his master.

"You shouldn't have done that," Willie said, running along beside them. "The poor dog's got a bur in his back." The boy leaned over and pulled the bur off the dog's back. It came out of the short hair easily. Willie was surprised to see that, instead of growling, Brutus wagged his tail.

Brutus and Hulk Hoskins returned to the striped tent, and Willie went slowly back to the campfire with the bur still in his hand. After Hulk Hoskins had gone into his tent, Willie heard the tiger begin to roar. It occurred to him that the tiger had not roared at all while Hulk Hoskins was out of his tent. But Willie did not waste much time thinking about the tiger.

The highly trained dogs crowded around Willie, wagging their tails and eager to be praised for their good behavior.

Absentmindedly Willie gave each one a friendly pat. He kept feeling the prickle of the bur that he held in his hand. He remembered how Sancho's shaggy coat had been full of burs last night. Brutus had short hair and burs would not easily stick to it. Yet one had been stuck there where he could not pull it off. Had the two dogs been to the same place?

"I wonder?" Willie said to himself.

The highly trained dogs were all watching him, as if to ask what next.

Liddy stood on her hind legs and put her front paws against Willie's knee. Tip rolled over three times, and Prince and Grushenka bounded away and then returned, as if they wanted Willie to go somewhere with them.

"You are right," Willie said. "We must try to see and speak with Professor Petit. Although he can't get out of prison, perhaps he can advise us what to do."

Professor Petit looked sadly out of his prison window and saw Willie and the four highly trained dogs below him. The dogs all barked with delight and wagged their tails at sight of their master. Sancho came to the window and stood on his hind legs with his paws on the windowsill. He poked his nose through the bars and barked back at his comrades.

"Well, Professor," said Willie politely, "how goes it?"

"Not too badly," said the professor. "I have had time to think, and Sancho has had time to rest and regain his cheerful spirits. Is there any news?"

"Yes," said Willie. "Hulk Hoskins offers to pay your debts for you, but in return he expects to take the caravan, the pony, and these four dogs and add them to his show."

"Ah!" said Professor Petit. "But that must never happen, Willie. Never!"

"I know," said Willie. "We must get out of our troubles in some better way than that."

"First of all," said Professor Petit, "I want to prove

that Sancho did not do this wicked thing. If he could only *speak*!"

"How are you, my friend?" said Sancho happily.

"He does not know what is in store for him, poor dog! There is only one slender hope," continued the professor. "Bring me Sancho's alphabet box, Willie, and we shall see if he can spell out something for us. There is scarcely one chance in ten thousand that he will be able to tell us anything, but it is worth taking that one chance."

# 10

## SANCHO'S ALPHABET

When Professor Petit had spoken, the four free dogs began to leap about Willie and beg him to hurry. They dashed along beside him to help carry out their master's orders. When they saw that Willie was taking Sancho's alphabet box from the caravan, they came to the conclusion that a show was about to be given. Liddy pulled out her ladder and Tip helped her to drag it along. Prince pulled out the basket in which he carried Liddy during a performance. Grushenka ran here and there hunting for her ball. Unfortunately the ball was packed away with the costumes and she could not find it. However, in a corner of the caravan she found the ball of rope which Professor Petit stretched across between the ladders for Liddy to walk on. It rolled almost as well as a ball, and Grushenka caught it up in her mouth and trotted away after Willie and the other dogs.

Willie went to the front door of the prison to see the jailer. But the dogs all ran around beneath Professor Petit's window to show their master that they were ready for a performance.

"Take a box to one of the prisoners?" cried the jailer when Willie wished to hand him Sancho's box. "Of course not! How do I know that it does not contain a saw or a couple of bed sheets or a pistol or a rope? I couldn't think of taking a box to one of the prisoners."

"But look," said Willie, "it has nothing but alphabet blocks in it. There is not the least bit of harm in the box. Please give it to Professor Petit."

"No," said the jailer. "This man is a magician of some kind with his sheep killers and his talking dogs. I'll admit that the blocks look innocent enough, but they are probably full of keys or small bottles of poison or other wicked magic. No, indeed! I'll not run the risk of giving *anything* to the prisoner."

In vain Willie argued, and at last he was obliged to give up any thought of getting Sancho's box to Professor Petit by way of the jailer. He went around to the side of the prison to tell the showman his difficulties and there were the dogs, with ladder, basket and rope ball, waiting to begin their performance.

"Alas, Professor!" said Willie. "I don't know how I am to get the blocks up to you. The jailer refuses to take them, and your window is too high to reach."

"Think a moment," said the professor. "The dogs are ready to help you."

Willie looked around, thinking as hard as he could.

There was a large tree in the prison yard, but even if he could climb it, the tree was not quite near enough to Professor Petit's window for Willie to be able to pass the box to him. The box was also too large to be handed through the bars.

The dogs stood around Willie wagging their tails and wishing to be helpful.

"If Grushenka could toss the ball of rope over the branch of the tree," Willie said, "while Tip held one end of it in his mouth—"

"Yes, yes," said the professor.

"And then," continued Willie, "if Prince, holding the other end of the rope in his teeth, could jump high enough for you to catch hold of that end of the rope—"

"Yes."

"Then you could fasten your end of the rope to one of the bars of the window—"

"Yes."

"And then I could make Tip's end of the rope quite fast to the tree, so that the rope was stretched tight between the tree and the prison window."

"Yes, yes!" said Professor Petit excitedly.

"And then I could hold Liddy's ladder up against the tree, and she could climb up to the tightrope and walk across."

"That's right! That's it! It can be done!"

"But Professor," Willie cried, "Liddy could never carry the box across the tightrope, and you could not get it through the bars, if she did."

"Try her with the basket, Willie," cried the professor. "Put only a few blocks in the basket at once. She will have to make several trips across the rope."

It was a difficult thing to do, but the dogs were wonderfully helpful. At Willie's command Grushenka began tossing up the ball of rope under the branch of the tree while Tip held one end of the rope in his mouth. Each time the rope ball fell back, it tangled and unwound, and Willie was obliged to rewind it and ask the dogs to try again. Willie tried to toss it up himself, but he was not able to send it as high as Grushenka could. She balanced the ball on her nose, made a great leap into the air, at the same time tossing with her head, and the ball really soared. At the fifth try, the ball went over the limb and came down in a shower of rope on the other side.

Now, at Willie's direction, Prince took up the end of the rope in his teeth and began to leap upward toward the prison window. Prince was larger and could leap much higher than Grushenka although he did not have her skill at tossing a ball.

Professor Petit thrust his hand out of the prison window between the bars, and as Prince made his most prodigious leap into the air, the professor was able to grasp the rope and hold it. Now Willie made Tip's end of the rope fast to the tree trunk, and the professor tied his end of the rope securely around one of the window bars. The rope was stretched between the limb of the tree and the prison window.

When Liddy saw the rope stretched tight, she began to bark and dance about with eagerness to perform her act. But first Willie put a few of the alphabet blocks into the basket.

"How many blocks do you think she can carry, Professor?"

"The basket is large and heavy," said the professor. "We must not expect too much of her. Let me see, there are twenty-six letters in the alphabet. Let us discard x and z, which are not very useful letters in spelling, and that will leave twenty-four blocks. Now, if she could carry six blocks at each trip, she would have to make only four trips across the rope. Try six blocks, Willie."

Liddy took the handle of the basket in her mouth, and, with six blocks in it, she was able to carry it easily with her four feet on the ground.

"But will she be able to carry it across a tightrope so high in the air? And, if she should fall, won't she hurt herself?" Willie wondered.

"It is dangerous," Professor Petit said, "but I think she can do it. However, Willie, take off your jacket and let Prince and Grushenka hold it by its edges in their mouths, so that, if she falls, the outstretched jacket will act as a net to break her fall."

Willie did as the professor advised. Prince and Grushenka were stationed beneath the tightrope, holding Willie's outspread jacket. Tip was given the basket to hand up to Willie as soon as it was needed. Willie put Liddy up on his shoulder and then raised the ladder against the tree. Liddy stepped upon the first rung of the ladder and, while Willie held the ladder in place with one hand, he reached down with the other hand, took the basket from Tip, and handed it to Liddy. Liddy took the handle of the basket in her mouth and began to climb the ladder. She went very slowly for the heavy basket bumped against the rungs of the ladder as she went up. The dogs were all very silent and tense. They felt the importance of the act and the difficulty of bringing it to a successful conclusion.

Slowly Liddy climbed to the limb of the tree. She rested there a few moments, looking down at Willie and the three dogs and then across at her master and

Sancho. She shivered a little and shook herself. Then she wagged her tail, and stepped out very daintily onto the stretched rope, carrying the basket in her mouth. The rope swayed under her weight, but the little dog kept her balance. She began to go forward very cautiously, one foot ahead of another foot until she was halfway across the rope. There a sudden trembling seized her and she paused as if she wished to turn around and retrace her steps. Prince and Grushenka stood staunchly below, holding the coat to catch her. Willie and Tip remained perfectly still, unable to breathe freely until she should reach the other side.

"Come, Liddy. Come, my girl," said Professor Petit very softly. "I know that you can do it."

With a little rush of confidence Liddy suddenly moved forward, and in a moment she was safe on the window ledge, still holding the basket in her mouth.

The professor was able to rest the basket on the ledge while he removed the blocks. Then he patted the little dog on the head and she covered his hand with kisses. She was so pleased with herself that she almost wiggled off the narrow window sill.

"You have done very nobly, Liddy," Professor Petit said, "but you must remain calm, for your work is not yet completed." He put the empty basket into her mouth, and she returned slowly across the rope to the tree and the ladder. Willie had another six blocks ready to put into the basket, and so the little dog made three more perilous journeys to and fro across the rope. When all the blocks except x and z had been transported, the friends could draw easy breath again. Willie put on his jacket, and the four highly trained dogs frisked and barked.

Up in the prison cell they heard Sancho barking also. He was very much delighted to have his blocks again and to be able to spell and do his arithmetic problems.

Now Willie leaned against the tree, looking upward toward the window. Grushenka and Liddy sat on one side of him with their tongues hanging out. Prince and Tip sat on the other side of him with *their* tongues hanging out. They all looked up at the window awaiting news.

At intervals the professor looked out of the window to tell them what progress he was making.

"I have arranged the blocks," he said, "and Sancho is looking at them. To get him into the proper frame of mind, I shall ask him to spell his name and several other words that he knows."

In a few moments the professor reported: "He has spelled his name. He has spelled *cat*, *dog*, and *man*. Now I shall ask him a question whose answer he has not been taught."

The other four dogs had begun to lie down now, still panting and looking anxiously up at the window. Then they heard Professor Petit's voice asking Sancho the question that he had not been taught.

*"Who killed Farmer Olney's sheep?"*

There was a long pause, during which the question was repeated several times. Then Professor Petit said: "He has selected the letter B."

The four dogs sat up again, and Willie felt the hair prickling all over his head. *He is going to tell us!* he thought.

"R," reported the professor.

"BR," said Willie softly.

"U," said Professor Petit.

"BRU," repeated Willie.

"T," said the professor.

"BRUT," repeated Willie. His heart began to pound. He could feel the bur in his pocket that had come from Brutus's back. Would Sancho really tell them who had killed the farmer's sheep?

But now there came a longer pause than any before.

"He will not go on," Professor Petit said. "Something has confused him. He is very much disturbed. I think we must start all over again."

In vain the blocks were rearranged and the question

repeated. Sancho picked out four letters, BRUT, and then he became confused, and finally rolled over onto his back, pretending to be dead.

"Alas!" said Professor Petit, "I am afraid that we have proved nothing. My good little dog has tried his best. But how could I expect him to spell words that I had never taught him?"

"But the name *Brutus*," Willie cried. "He might know that word, Professor, because it is spelled out in large letters on Brutus's collar. Sancho has seen it many times."

"That is true," said the professor, "but, you see, he does not spell *Brutus*, only BRUT. We may just as well imagine he is trying to spell *brute*."

"Then perhaps it is the tiger he has in mind," said Willie hopefully.

"No, my dear Willie," said the professor. "One must learn to accept defeat as gracefully as possible. My dog is willing, but the fact remains that the letters he has selected do not spell anything. We can try again tomorrow when he is rested, but I believe that we shall have to find some better way of proving his innocence than this."

The four dogs seemed to sense the general disappointment. They followed Willie slowly back to the caravan with their tails at half-mast.

# THE OFFER REFUSED

**H**ulk Hoskins's Show was still in town the next day. He had not yet let the people of Puddling Center see enough of his tiger to satisfy them, and so they were willing to keep buying tickets for each new show, hoping to see more.

Hulk Hoskins rubbed his hands together with delight and jingled the money in his pockets. He came to the caravan as Willie and the highly trained dogs were having breakfast.

"Well," said he, "did you give my message to Professor Petit?"

"Yes, I did," said Willie.

"And what did he say?"

"He refused your offer."

"*Refused?*" cried Mr. Hoskins, growing red with anger. "He refused my kind and generous offer to help him out of his troubles?"

"He refused your offer," repeated Willie. It did not seem necessary to add the "kind and generous" part.

"Then let him rot in prison," said Hulk Hoskins, "and I fully expect that they will shoot his dog as a sheep killer and a disturber of the peace."

"Mr. Hoskins," said Willy, "I'd just like to know where Brutus was at the time when Farmer Olney's sheep were killed."

"Brutus?" said the showman in surprise. "But Brutus is always with me."

"Not always," said Willie, "for I myself have seen him roaming free at evening, hunting for food."

"Well, it is no use trying to pin this deed on Brutus," said Hulk Hoskins, "for there is not a shred of evidence against him."

"Don't be too sure of that, Mr. Hoskins," said Willie. He took the bur out of his pocket and held it up delicately between his thumb and forefinger. "I have this."

Hulk Hoskins looked at the bur and his eyes narrowed. But then he began to laugh his unpleasant laugh.

"A bur!" he said. "The fields are full of them, and any dog might have one in his coat. A sorry bit of evidence. Ha! Ha!"

Soon after Mr. Hoskins had returned to his tent, Willie had another visitor to the caravan, and it was Uncle Scrivens.

"Now, Willie," said Uncle Scrivens, "I need you, as usual, at the post office. I've been very patient about this affair of the highly trained dogs. But I don't know what your poor, dear mother would say if she knew you were the comrade of a man who is in jail."

"Why, Uncle," said Willie stoutly, "Mother would be glad to see that I'm loyal to a friend, and the more so because he is in trouble."

"Well, I think you are out of your senses, lad. But the thing can't go on much longer, for I understand that Professor Petit and his sheep-killing dog are to be tried this morning."

"This morning?" Willie cried. "So soon?"

"Yes," said Uncle Scrivens. "The trial has been set for this morning, so that nobody will have to miss seeing Hoskins's tiger this afternoon. As far as I am concerned, I have paid out the last shilling I care to part with to look at the tiger. A flash of orange and black through a flaming hoop, and that's all Hoskins lets you see of his tiger. Hoskins is a smart man. He'll be rich. But I'm a smart man also—too smart to lose my shillings for nothing."

"Uncle," Willie said, seizing Mr. Scrivens's hand, "there's something about you that I can't help liking after all."

"I'm sure I don't know what it is," said Uncle Scrivens crossly. "And I suppose now you'll insist on going to this trial and not delivering my letters."

"Oh, yes," said Willy. "I'm going to the trial, but I'll deliver the letters for you this afternoon if you can wait so long."

It did not really matter that the letters were not delivered in the morning, because everybody in town had come to the courthouse to see Professor Petit's trial. Nothing else was thought of. Even Miss Charmian and the children came down from school to be present.

"For," said Miss Charmian, "this is the first trial Puddling Center has had in years, and it should be very educational for the children."

Instead of walking sedately two by two, or even skipping as they had done the last time, Willie was amazed to see that the children came down from school waltzing in couples. Troubled as he was about the fate of Sancho and Professor Petit, Willie could not help thinking, "This is Tip's doing. He has taught them how to waltz."

The courtroom was crowded when Willie and the four dogs entered. Willie had carefully brushed and groomed the dogs and put on their costumes, so that they would look their best in honor of their master. They came down the aisle behind Willie, wagging their tails and hanging out their tongues, for they confidently supposed that this was some new sort of performance. The people in the courtroom all turned around and craned their necks to see. Some jostled and others stood on tiptoe to look at the marvelous dogs.

"As good as Hoskins's tiger!" someone said.

"Better," said someone else, "for *this* we can really see, and it doesn't take a penny out of pocket."

There was room left on the very front bench, and here Willie sat himself down with the dogs beside him. Prince sat up straight and tall with Grushenka next to him. Liddy, in her plumed bonnet, fidgeted after a flea, and Tip soon curled up and went to sleep. Still the dogs were a handsome sight, and more than one person said, "Sure, such well-behaved dogs would never chase sheep."

"But it's the other one—the black one—that did the mischief."

"Nay, he's a highly trained dog also. I can't believe that any one of them would be up to such wickedness."

When the judge entered, everyone in the courtroom arose. Willie spoke to the highly trained dogs and they all stood up on their hind legs, although they did not know for what reason. Even Tip uncurled himself and stood up with only one eye open and the other eye still asleep. But he was doing his best.

"Bring in the prisoners," said the judge, when all were seated again.

The dogs pricked up their ears as Professor Petit and Sancho were led into the courtroom, and they began to bark with pleasure. Liddy was all for jumping down to run to her waltzing partner. But Willie said: "Down, friends! Sit! Quiet now! Behave yourselves." So the dogs sat quietly, but their ears were pricked forward and their noses wiggled with the pleasure of recognition.

# THE TRIAL

After two nights in prison, Professor Petit and Sancho lacked the smart air of grooming that the rest of the troupe had. They seemed tired and discouraged. But Willie noted with satisfaction that Professor Petit's pockets and shirt front bulged with small, squarish lumps.

*He has brought the alphabet blocks with him*, Willie thought. *That can only mean that he still hopes Sancho will tell us something.*

"Now," said the judge, "what is the charge against these prisoners?"

"Your honor, sir," said Farmer Olney, standing up and speaking loudly, "I charge this here dog with feloniously and wickedly running two of my sheep all around the pasture and then biting their throats so that their blood ran out and they died."

"And what makes you think it was this particular dog?" asked the judge.

"Because," said Farmer Olney, "he was my sheep herder. Willie used to herd sheep for me, and then he brought me this highly trained dog to do the job so that he'd have time to go to school. 'Tis so, Willie?"

"Yes, sir," Willie said, standing up and speaking out plainly. All of the dogs looked up at Willie and wagged their tails as he spoke. "Yes, sir. We apprenticed four of the highly trained dogs to work in my place so that I might go to school. Three of them have given perfect satisfaction, your honor. You may ask the baker, the weaver, and the miller if these dogs have not worked well. They will tell you yes."

"We shall have the testimony of the baker, the weaver, and the miller in a few moments," said the judge, "but now we'll hear what the farmer has to say."

"Yes, sir, your honor," Willie said, "but I just wanted to put in here that Sancho was herding the sheep as well as the other dogs were doing their jobs, and I don't believe he's guilty of any wrong."

"Order in the court!" cried the judge, pounding on his desk with a small wooden hammer which is called a gavel. "We haven't got around to personal opinions yet. Now, Mr. Olney, proceed. Proceed, Mr. Olney, proceed."

"My seeding is done for the year, sir," said Mr. Olney, "but this I can tell you, my two sheep are as dead as posts, and what I want is this. I want this dog to be shot, so he won't kill any more sheep, and I want that his master pay me twenty-five dollars for my two sheep and the mental anguish I have suffered. And the sooner 'tis all settled, the better."

"Now, now," said the judge, "we must not go too fast, Farmer Olney. For there is this strange thing about the law, that a man (and a dog, too, I suppose, although it's never happened to come up before, to my certain knowledge) that a man is presumed to be innocent until someone has proved him guilty. Now who is to prove this dog guilty?"

"Your honor," cried Farmer Olney, "maybe you don't get the drift of my remarks, but that there is exactly what I'm trying to prove. This dog herds my sheep; he brings them back, two missing; later, I find the two lying dead in the fields. When I go to seek this dog, I find him resting by his master's fire plumb played out, and his coat all full of burs. It's as plain as the nose on your face."

"Let's have the prisoner into the witness box," said the judge.

The jailer thrust Sancho into the witness box, but

at the same time he cried out, "But, your honor, he can't speak."

"How are you, my friend?" said Sancho in a pleasant voice. The judge almost fell out of his chair at the sound of these words from the mouth of a dog. There was a sigh of astonishment from the spectators, then a growing murmur of wonder and respect.

"Let him tell his side of it. Let him defend himself," voices said.

Now Professor Petit arose, and Willie could see that he was pale and nervous.

"Your honor," the professor said to the judge, "my good dog has learned only these few words. He could not possibly defend himself with his own voice. But he does have a certain skill in spelling. If you will allow me, I'll put his spelling blocks before him, and you may question him. I cannot promise you how well he will be able to answer your questions. But we can at least try."

A whisper of awe and astonishment went around the room. The judge pulled his gown about his shoulders and settled himself securely into his chair.

"What is your name, dog?" he inquired.

Very quickly and expertly the little black dog picked out the letters S A N C H O and put them in order before the judge. The people stood on tiptoe to see, their mouths open with wonder.

"And what is your age?" Sancho turned over the blocks with his paw until he found the 3. This he took in his mouth and laid before the judge.

"Is it true that he is three years old?" asked the judge, looking at Professor Petit.

"Quite true," said the professor. "In other words he is of legal age, for they say that every year of a dog's life is equal to seven years in the life of a man."

"Now, Sancho," said the judge in an impressive voice, *"who killed Farmer Olney's sheep?"*

There was a moment's pause. The courtroom was perfectly silent. With his tail curled up behind him, Sancho sat quiet. Willie thought that he looked puzzled, but, when the judge repeated the question, the dog pricked his ears forward and began slowly and delicately to push the letters about with his paw.

First he selected a B, then an R, then a U, and then a T. At that he stopped. His tongue hung out as if he had been running a race. He looked all around him and wagged his tail apologetically. Then he lay down and rolled over on his back with his eyes closed and his legs in the air.

"Go on! Go on!" the people in the courtroom cried. "He is trying to spell Brutus, but why doesn't he finish it?"

"Your honor," cried Willie, jumping to his feet. "I am sure that it was Brutus who killed the sheep. Here is a bur that I found on his back. It is the same kind of bur that was found on Sancho's coat. In my opinion Sancho was trying to protect the sheep from Brutus. In my opinion Brutus is the killer."

"Will somebody please keep that boy in his seat?" roared the judge. "I don't want opinions, I want facts. If this highly trained dog had spelled BRUTUS, we might have something to go on. But BRUT spells nothing at all. It is simply a chance selection of letters that have no meaning."

"I am not so sure of that, your honor," said Professor Petit. "I have asked my dog this same question many times. He does not make a chance selection. He always chooses the same four letters and then he lies down in confusion unable to go on."

Just then Miss Charmian arose at the back of the courtroom. Her cheeks were pink with embarrassment, but her voice was quite clear. The children all looked at her proudly as she said:

"Your honor, I should like to point out that there is only one U in the alphabet. If he is trying to spell Brutus, no wonder he is confused, for where in the world is he going to find another U?"

In an instant the courtroom was in an uproar.

"Where is Brutus?" the people cried. "Brutus ought to be shot."

In vain the judge hammered for silence. At last he dismissed court for lack of evidence.

"This does not mean that the case is ended," he said. "Professor Petit and Sancho must be returned to jail until we are able to gather more facts and look further into this matter. Brutus and his master must also be questioned, for now they are equally under suspicion. As soon as they have finished their afternoon show, we shall put them under arrest."

The policeman and the jailer beamed with delight. *Two* men and *two* dogs in jail at one time! This was a rare treat for the serious people of Puddling Center. It was quite as exciting as having two shows in town at once.

Only Willie was disturbed.

"Wouldn't it be better to arrest them right away?" he said to Uncle Scrivens. "Why should they wait until Hulk Hoskins has given another show? He might very well escape if he hears what they intend to do."

"My dear nephew," replied Uncle Scrivens, "naturally it is because of the tiger. Even the judge wishes to have another view of the tiger before he puts Hulk Hoskins under arrest."

Willie waved his hand at Professor Petit and Sancho, before the jailer led them away. He thought that the professor looked more hopeful than he had looked at any time since his arrest. Willie turned toward the caravan with Prince, Grushenka, and Liddy trotting beside him. Tip had disappeared, but soon he rejoined them, carrying the judge's gavel in his mouth. Willie was obliged to take the gavel away from Tip and return it, with apologies, to the judge.

"Tip," he said severely, "we are in trouble enough without any help from you." But Tip only frisked and wagged his tail, and it was clear to see that he did not feel he had done wrong.

# 13

# TIP'S BAD DAY

Willie made up his mind that, come what might, he would attend Hoskins's Circus that afternoon. It was not that he still yearned to gaze at the tiger. Too many more important matters occupied his mind for that. But he felt that someone with the interests of Professor Petit at heart should be there to keep an eye on Hulk Hoskins in case he tried to slip away and escape arrest.

The next question was what to do with the highly trained dogs while he attended the circus. He did not like to leave them alone, even shut in the caravan, for there was so much feeling for and against them in Puddling Center that he could not be sure they would be safe.

"If I could be certain that they would behave themselves, I'd take them with me," Willie said. He did not realize that he had spoken aloud until he saw that three of the dogs had come to sit around him, attentively awaiting instructions. It was as if they said, "Try us; we promise to be good."

"But where is Tip?" asked Willie, looking for the fourth dog. As he spoke, Willie saw Tip coming from the direction of Hulk Hoskins's tent with an object in his mouth.

"Another tent peg, I suppose," remarked Willie patiently. "That naughty Tip has chewed up enough pegs from Hoskins's tent to make it quite possible for anyone to crawl under the flap and enter by the back way." He ran to take the tent peg away from Tip before the little dog should begin to chew it. But Tip was tired of having things taken away from him. He dodged this way and that, keeping just out of reach. Barking with pleasure, Prince, Grushenka, and Liddy joined in the chase. After the tedious morning in the courtroom they were all ready for an active game. In vain Willie tried to convince them that this was a serious matter, but they could not believe him. Away they ran, helter-skelter all around the square, leaping into the air and barking happily.

Finally, to escape his pursuers, Tip ran in under the green caravan. Steps were let down at the back when the caravan was not in motion, and under these

Tip crawled, so that the others could not get at him.

"Well, it's only a tent peg," Willie said, as he knelt down to look under the steps. He could see Tip's mischievous eyes looking out at him from the shadows. But was it a tent peg that he had in his mouth? It was a rather long, limp object with stripes running around it.

"For goodness' sake!" Willie said to himself, "if I didn't know that such a thing was impossible, I'd say he had stolen the tiger's tail."

He knew, however, that this was out of the question, for he could hear the tiger roaring as usual. The roar was no louder, no softer than it had been before. Surely a tiger who had lost his tail would roar more terribly than he had ever roared before. Willie was puzzled. He tried to coax Tip out of his dark corner. But Tip only lay there, quietly chewing on the end of his long, limp striped object, and his eyes seemed to laugh at Willie from the dark shadows.

Willie was obliged to leave him there while he ran off to deliver the letters. Prince ran to the baker's, Grushenka to the weaver's, and Liddy to the miller's, and thus the work of the town was carried on as usual.

Tip was very bad that day. When Willie returned and groomed the other dogs for their appearance at the circus, Tip continued to lie under the caravan steps with his prize. Liddy crawled under the steps beside him, but even she could not induce him to come out.

"Well, we'll go without him," Willie said.

From the other side of the square the barrel organ could be heard grinding out its mechanical tune. At regular intervals the tiger roared. Because they understood that this was likely to be the last display of the tiger before Hulk Hoskins was arrested, the people of Puddling Center turned out in crowds.

Willie and the three dogs passed into the tent with the crowd, but Willie was obliged to pay four shillings and four pennies. No one got into Hoskins's Circus free—not even a dog.

There was an air of tension and excitement in the tent that afternoon. Willie thought that Mr. Hoskins looked nervous and somewhat less shiny than he had looked at former performances. Surely the lamplight was as bright as ever, but the medals, the earrings, the gold braid and flashing teeth and eyes of the ringmaster were less dazzling than before. Hulk Hoskins kept looking around him as if he were in search of something. It was almost time for Brutus's act, and suddenly Willie noticed another thing.

"Brutus is not here!" Willie said to himself.

"Mr. Hoskins is looking for Brutus." A number of speculations ran through Willie's mind. Brutus had been sent away to escape arrest. If so, that might prove that he was guilty of killing the sheep. But, if Hulk Hoskins had sent Brutus away, why should he seem to be looking for him? Or perhaps Farmer Olney had decided to take the law into his own hands and had done away with Brutus. Willie looked all around and he saw that Farmer Olney was not in the audience. But still Willie could not believe that this was so, either, because Farmer Olney had seemed convinced that Sancho was the sheep killer. Why should he destroy Brutus until he was sure that Brutus was guilty?

As Willie was thinking these various thoughts, the three dogs beside him began to growl very deep in their throats. He could see the hair rising along their backs. He spoke to them softly, putting his hands on their backs to quiet them. And he knew at once that Brutus must have come into the tent.

*It is strange that they will growl at Brutus while the nearness of the tiger does not bother them*, Willie thought. To the dogs he said, "Quiet, friends. Be still. You must be good now." He was glad after all that Tip had not come, since it was Tip's day for being naughty. He was sure that Prince, Grushenka, and Liddy would behave themselves if he wished it.

He saw now that Brutus had come through the red curtains at the back of the stage just in time to join his master for his part of the performance. His tongue was lolling out, and his sides heaved, as if he had been running for a long time. But apparently he had recently been fed, for his usually lean stomach was bulging cozily.

Hulk Hoskins cracked his whip, and Willie could see Brutus flinch as if he knew all too well how the whip felt on his back. In spite of himself Willie was sorry for Brutus. He could pity any dog who has a cruel master.

Brutus seized the leather strap in his teeth. The barrel organ played, the winch creaked as Hulk Hoskins turned it. Slowly the dog was lifted to the top of the tent.

"Ah-h-h!" murmured the people in the audience as they always did at this display of Brutus's strength. Their eyes were all turned upward to the top of the tent where Brutus was suspended by his teeth. Only Willie did not look at Brutus, but at Hoskins's face. Mr. Hoskins had his hand on the handle of the winch, but he was not looking at Brutus either. His eyes stared up the central aisle of the tent between the rows of seats, and on his face there dawned a look of surprise and astonishment which rapidly changed to one of horror. The cruel black eyes bulged; the mouth fell open in consternation. Hulk Hoskins's hand faltered on the handle of the winch.

Willie glanced behind him to see what had suddenly terrified the showman, and all he could see was Tip, trotting quietly down the aisle with something in his mouth. The something was long and limp and striped. It looked very much like the tail of a tiger, but it certainly could not be that, for a wisp of straw was sticking out of the end of it.

# 14.

# FIRE! FIRE!

Everything happened very rapidly after that. Hulk Hoskins gave a loud cry and let go of the handle of the winch. The rope that held Brutus suspended at the top of the tent began suddenly to unroll, letting him fall like a plummet. As he felt himself falling, the great dog kicked out his legs in an effort to save himself. His legs struck the lamp that hung from the tent top. The lamp swung perilously, and in an instant, the top of the tent had caught fire. People began to scream and rush for the exit. Willie saw that what had only a moment before been a popular spectacle was rapidly turning into a death trap.

Willie sprang out of his seat, and cried to the people: "Stop! Stop! You will harm yourselves more by crowding than by taking your time!"

To the dogs, he cried, *"Fetch water! Fetch ladder! Fire! Fire!"*

Away the dogs raced, dashing under the back edge of the tent at the place where Tip had carried off the tent pegs. It was still Tip's bad day, however, and he paid no attention to Willie's command. He continued up the aisle and onto the platform beneath the flaming top. With the long, striped object still in his mouth, he got up on hind legs and began to waltz.

"Look!" Willie cried to the people. "The show is going on. Don't crowd. Don't push! Stop and watch the show, and there will be plenty of time for all of you to get out in an orderly way."

The panic began to subside and the audience to stop and look at Tip before rushing into a stampede at the narrow exit.

Voices cried: "Fire! Fire!" and "Help! Help!" and among the various cries of distress, one excited voice cried out: "He's got the tiger's tail in his mouth. It's stuffed with straw! We've all been tricked and defrauded! Look, will you!"

Now there arose a very pandemonium of cries. Some people were trying to escape the fire; others were trying to get their hands on Hulk Hoskins. But in the smoke and confusion nobody could find the owner of the show. From behind the red curtain came the chatter of the frightened monkeys and the growling of the bear. Yet strangely enough, in this moment of emergency, the tiger had forgotten to roar. There was only silence from the most terrible of beasts.

Willie ran to the back of the tent and propped up the flap where the tent pegs were missing. He could see Prince and Grushenka running up from the river, carrying buckets of water which they emptied into the red fire cart. At the cry of "Fire!" and the activity of the dogs, the pony had left his daisies and buttercups and was eagerly pawing the ground beside the red fire cart. Willie ran across the square and slipped the harness over the pony's head. Liddy hopped to her place beside the ladders and Grushenka jumped up beside the pump. Prince dashed away again to the river with the empty pail in his mouth.

Now Willie caught the pony's bridle and ran with him toward the burning tent. The bell on the red cart clanged; the pony trotted. Excited and eager, Liddy and Grushenka clung to the cart as it jogged across the square. Oh, for Sancho's help now! If only Prince could carry enough water to keep the pump filled!

By now the top of the tent was burning briskly. A glance showed Willie that the people were all safely out, but he could still hear the chattering of the monkeys and the growling of the bear. They were chained behind the red curtains and could not help themselves. They must certainly be saved, and also the tiger. Willie's mind was in a hopeless state of confusion. Was there a tiger after all? And was he worth saving?

There was no time to be lost now in speculation. Willie halted the pony as near to the burning tent as possible. This was not such an easy matter as extinguishing the fire in the little house. Here Liddy and Grushenka could not manage the ladder by themselves. Willie had to raise it and hold it in position for Liddy to climb. She began to climb, as he held the ladder, carrying the nozzle of the hose in her mouth. Grushenka began to pump. Prince came running from the river with another bucket of water suspended from his mouth. The water splashed into the tank on the red cart, as Prince tipped it up.

"Someone must help him get water," Willie called to the crowd which was beginning to gather around them. As he spoke he heard more water splashing into the tank, and, looking around, he saw that another dog had taken Sancho's bucket and was helping Prince to keep the tank filled. With the greatest astonishment, Willie recognized Brutus. Brutus and Prince were working side by side without snarling or quarreling.

People from nearby houses now began to arrive with buckets to help the two dogs. Grushenka bobbed up and down at the pump. Out of the hose came a stream of water. Liddy held it firmly pointed at the flaming tent as she stood at the top of her ladder. There was a hiss and a crackle, a crackle and a hiss as water and fire met. Smoke began to replace the flame. Gradually the fire came under control. The tent was blackened and charred, but the flames had been stopped before they reached the trapped animals.

As soon as he could safely lower Liddy's ladder, Willie ran to the back of the stage, and parted the scorched red curtains. He flung them wide so that everyone could see. There were the poor, sad monkeys, chattering with fear; there was the bear, pacing back and forth and straining at the end of his chain. There was the tiger—Willie stepped back at the sight of him, for he was not confined in a cage. But the tiger did not move, and slowly Willie began to go toward him. The tiger's mouth was open, showing sharp teeth; there was a faint gleam in his eye. But no sound came out of the mouth, and the eyes did not move.

Willie took another step forward and put his hand on the tiger's head. Yes, the fur was real, but the eyes were made of glass, and the tiger's skin had been stuffed with straw. Willie's eye ran down the striped back and he saw that the tail was missing. A short bark at his side made him look down, and there sat Tip, looking up at Willie with something like a smile. One ear was cocked up and one down, and from Tip's mouth there still hung a remnant of the tiger's tail.

People began to gather from all sides now, looking at the stuffed tiger with anger and astonishment. "But we heard it roar!" they said.

Willie saw a mechanical device on the other side of the tiger which looked something like a music box. A handle stuck out of it, and now Willie gave the handle several turns. First there was a kind of whirring sound, and then the roar began. It was the roar which had so often struck terror into their hearts. At first the people stepped back in alarm. Then, seeing that the noise did not really come out of the tiger's mouth, they crowded close again.

"But he jumped through a hoop!" they cried. "We saw him jump through a hoop!"

Willie was puzzled, too. He had certainly seen the tiger jump through the flaming hoop with his own eyes. He walked all around the stuffed tiger, looking very carefully. Suddenly he noticed a lever which he took hold of and pulled sharply back. As he did so, a spring was released, and the mechanical tiger leapt forward in a half arc to the other side of the stage. If one saw it leap from curtain to curtain with the flaming hoop to dazzle the eyes, one would not know whether it had actually passed through the hoop or not, and the mechanical figure would certainly have given the appearance of being alive.

Suddenly Willie began to laugh. But the serious people of Puddling Center were not amused.

"Where is Hulk Hoskins?" they cried. "We'll tear him limb from limb! Where are his two assistants? They have tricked and defrauded us. They have taken our money, and worst of all, they have been laughing up their sleeves at us."

Hulk Hoskins and his two assistants had escaped during the confusion of the fire. They were nowhere to be seen. Their caravan and two horses had also vanished.

# 15

## FARMER OLNEY AGAIN

Just at this moment, when everyone was calling in vain for Hulk Hoskins, Farmer Olney came driving up to the tent in his high, two-wheeled cart. He was so full of some business of his own that he scarcely noticed the half-ruined tent and the excited crowd.

"Tell Hulk Hoskins to come out here," he bellowed. "I've business with this here Hoskins and his wicked dog. Send him out and let me talk to him."

"He's gone!" everybody cried. "Hoskins is gone. We can't find him."

"Then where's his dog?" the farmer roared. "Another of my sheep's been killed, and Sancho couldn't have done it, because Sancho's still in jail."

Willie looked around quickly and he saw that Brutus, with Sancho's bucket still near him, was sitting peaceably beside Prince and Grushenka as if he belonged in Professor Petit's troupe. He was just trying to scratch a bur from behind one ear as Willie looked at him.

"There's your culprit!" several people said. "There's Hulk Hoskins's dog!"

"By gum! He shall be shot!" cried Farmer Olney. "He's got a bur behind his ear, and I'd swear he's got a tag of sheep's wool sticking to that fancy collar of his!"

"Shoot Brutus!" everybody cried.

Willie thought very quickly. He could see that the serious people of Puddling Center were about to vent their anger at Hoskins upon his dog. It was probably true that Brutus had killed the farmer's sheep, but he had been hungry and ill-treated. Willie remembered what Professor Petit had said about a dog reflecting the character of his master.

"Just a minute," Willie cried, putting his hand on Brutus's collar so that he could not get away, and so that no one would harm him. "Remember that you are holding an innocent man and his dog in jail. Let Professor Petit out of jail, and he will tell us what we had better do with Brutus."

In a moment half of Puddling Center was on its way to the jail to release Professor Petit and Sancho.

The highly trained dogs ran ahead of Willie,

frisking and barking. Even Brutus trotted along, willingly enough, at the end of a leash.

Professor Petit and Sancho were looking anxiously out of the prison window. They had heard the cries of "Fire!", the clang of the bell on the red cart, the angry cries of the crowd. But from the high side window they could not see what was happening. Now, as the voices of the crowd drew near, they began to feel alarmed for their own safety.

"Justice!" Farmer Olney was shouting, and other voices cried out, "Let us have justice."

"Well," said Professor Petit to Sancho, "I only hope that 'justice' means doing the right thing by you and me, dear friend." Sancho barked a very cheerful reply, for just at that moment he had caught sight of the other highly trained dogs running ahead of the crowd. The four dogs began to leap over each other's backs and turn somersaults and roll over to show that they brought good news.

The jailer turned the great key in the lock and fetched the showman and his dog down from their cell.

"You are free, Professor Petit!" cried Willie. "Another of Farmer Olney's sheep has been killed, and, since Sancho was locked in jail, the farmer knows that Sancho could not have done it."

"It was this here Brutus all right!" cried Farmer Olney. "I'll have him shot, and I'll tan his blasted hide to make me a door mat."

"Not so fast, my good man," said Professor Petit. Willie saw that his friend the showman had already regained his poise and assurance, now that the prison walls lay behind him. "Not so fast, Mr. Olney; you have been very hasty about this whole matter."

"But I've lost three sheep!" wailed the farmer.

"That is true," said Professor Petit, "and you must certainly be repaid. But let us not replace one mistake by another because of haste. I see that you have captured Brutus. But where is Hulk Hoskins?"

It was explained to Professor Petit how the tent had caught fire, how the tiger had been exposed as a fraud, and how Hulk Hoskins and his two assistants had run away to escape the fury of the people.

Professor Petit thought for a few moments. His five dogs sat around him with their eyes fixed trustfully on his face. Brutus, too, came as close to Professor Petit as his leash would allow, and looked up into his face. The people of Puddling Center waited to hear what the professor would say.

"I think," said Professor Petit at last, "that we must indeed blame Brutus for the loss of Mr. Olney's sheep. But I should like to say this in his behalf, that he had a cruel master who did not teach him good manners nor give him enough to eat. An animal does not understand the difference between good and evil as a man does. Therefore we must not blame him too greatly, if he behaves no better than his master. Tell me, did Mr. Hoskins give you your money back, when you found out that the tiger was a fraud?"

"Our money!" cried the people of Puddling Center. "Where *is* our money?"

When they had hunted all over the half-burned tent and the place where Hoskins's caravan had stood without finding the box that contained their shillings and pennies, it was concluded that the dishonest showman had taken the money away with him.

Uncle Scrivens shook his head and said: "A smart man, Hoskins! But I can't help liking Professor Petit better."

Runners were dispatched in every direction to hunt for Hulk Hoskins, but by that time he was far ahead of them, and neither he, nor his two assistants, nor the bulk of the money that he had collected were ever seen again.

While the people were still hunting, however, one bag of the money was found. Tip came dragging it in, and it was all that he could do to pull it along beside him. His ears were cocked up with pride and his tail waved like a flag. Evidently the villains had dropped the bag in their flight, and Tip had discovered it as it lay by the wayside.

Professor Petit counted out the money in the bag and it came to nineteen dollars and fifty-four pence.

"Now," the professor said to the people of Puddling Center, "I could divide this money, which Tip has found, among all of you, but it would not begin to repay you for the money you paid to buy tickets to Hoskins's Circus. It is true that the circus turned out to be a fraud, and yet I am sure that you all had your money's worth of pleasure and excitement before you discovered that the tiger was stuffed with straw. Isn't this true?"

"Yes," the people admitted. "It was a very exciting week with two shows in town and all things else considered."

"Then," said the professor, "I should like to propose that we give this money to Farmer Olney to recompense him for the loss of his sheep. If he will forget his mental anguish, and will accept the remains of the tent, the plank seats, the hoop, and the red curtains as additional payment for the sheep, I believe that he will be amply rewarded."

Farmer Olney thought about this for a moment, scratching his head as he did so. He came to the conclusion that the offer was a fair one.

"But what about that dog?" he asked. "Won't he go right on chasing my sheep?"

"I believe not," said Professor Petit, "but, before we dispose of Brutus, let us consider the fate of the bear and the two monkeys."

The monkeys sat huddled together with their arms entwined. Occasionally one would pluck a flea from the fur of the other and crack it between his teeth. The bear sat up on his hind legs and mournfully rattled his chains.

"You could add them to your show," suggested Uncle Scrivens. "'Twould be a smart thing to do. You might get rich."

"No," said Professor Petit. "These are sad and unhappy animals. They need a permanent home among people who will be kind to them and help them to become happy again."

"Happy monkeys make folks laugh," said Willie, remembering something he had read about monkeys, who leapt about and swung by their tails.

"You are right, Willie," said Professor Petit, "and that brings me to my second point. Puddling Center is a very serious place. It has a jail, a courthouse, a post office, but nothing to make it laugh. It needs a zoo, and it needs the responsibility and pleasure of making animals happy in that zoo. The animals in turn will make the serious people of Puddling Center laugh. It will be a benefit all around."

While Uncle Scrivens, the judge, the miller, the weaver, and the baker hesitated, thinking this idea over, the children began to shout and beg.

"A zoo!" they cried. "We want a zoo!"

"It must be a large zoo," said Miss Charmian in her clear voice, "with lots of trees and grass and a warm little house for the winter. There will be no chains, of course, and there will be plenty of bananas and carrots and huckleberries to eat—"

"Yes! Yes!" cried the children.

In this way the matter was decided, quite simply and easily, and to the satisfaction of everybody.

# A FEW LAST WORDS

**B**ut how do you profit by all of this, Professor?" asked Uncle Scrivens. "Surely there is some-thing that you want for yourself. How about the tiger? You could go on showing him as Hoskins did. Just think of the money you would make!"

"No," replied the professor. "Mechanical things do not appeal to me. Perhaps I am old-fashioned, but I love to feel the breath of life in everything that surrounds me. Mechanical things are clever, but we must never pretend that they are as good as living things. And so the mechanical tiger may go on the junk heap as far as I am concerned. But I will take Brutus, if it is agreeable to all of you. I believe that I can make an honest and a clever dog of him, if I have a little time to train and educate him."

To Willie's surprise, he saw that Brutus was licking

Professor Petit's outstretched hand.

*And now the green caravan will be moving on,* thought Willie to himself. *How shall I ever bear to say good-bye to these dear friends of mine?* His face must have looked very downcast, for Professor Petit took him gently by the arm.

"Come along to the caravan, Willie," he said. "We'll talk things over, whilst I prepare the stew."

The dogs were all tired by the activities of the day. They lay about the fire with their heads resting on their outstretched paws. Tip even snored a little in his sleep. Brutus lay among them, as if he had always belonged to the troupe, and the other dogs seemed to accept him because their master did. There was a good odor of birch smoke and of cooking meat and vegetables on the evening air.

"You will not have to worry about the tiger anymore," Willie said. "The highly trained dogs will be the only show on the road, as well as the best one. Will you be leaving soon?"

"Early tomorrow morning," Professor Petit replied.

"Where will you go first?" Willie asked. His voice was tinged with sadness, although he tried hard to keep it cheerful.

"I figure to stop first at Wickersham," said Professor Petit briskly.

"Why, that's where I used to live!" said Willie in surprise. "My mother and my six brothers and sisters live near Wickersham."

"I know," said Professor Petit. "That's why we're going there, of course."

"We—?" faltered Willie.

"My dear Willie," said the professor, "the dogs and I would be very lonely without you, now that you have helped us through our days of distress. Surely you should also share in the success that I expect is coming to us. I thought that if you would come along with us as far as Wickersham, where we shall give our first show, we could see your mother and get her permission for you to join our troupe. I would pay you as fair a wage as our future success permits, and I would undertake your education as well. With all due respect to Miss Charmian, who is a most pleasant lady and who spoke out with great good sense on at least two important occasions—" (The professor cleared his throat here and looked as modest as it is possible for a brisk man to look.) "With all due respect to Miss Charmian, I say, I believe that you will find in Professor Pierre Petit a teacher of even wider knowledge."

Willie felt his heart beating more rapidly. To go with Professor Petit and the highly trained dogs on their travels! Nothing could possibly have pleased him more. But one thing still bothered him.

"But what will my uncle Scrivens do without a boy to run errands? And the miller, the baker, the weaver, and the farmer?"

"Liddy has cleared all the rats and mice out of the mill for the present," said Professor Petit, "and, if they return, the miller has only to turn the handle of the tiger's roaring machine to frighten them away. After all of his bad luck with his sheep, I believe that the farmer will prefer to do his own herding from now on. As for the baker, the weaver, and your uncle Scrivens, haven't you another brother, Willie, who might like to come to Puddling Center for a start in life?"

"There's Charlie," Willie said thoughtfully. "He's past ten. I believe he could handle the errands of Uncle Scrivens, the baker, and the weaver."

"Besides," said the professor, "I believe that there is going to be more pleasure and less serious work in Puddling Center from now on. Listen, Willie!" He held up a hand, and Willie listened.

From the other side of the square came the sound of the barrel organ and the shuffle of dancing feet.

"They're waltzing!" Willie exclaimed. "The Puddling Center people are waltzing!"

"Exactly," said Professor Petit, with a broad and pleasant smile. "It's what they've been secretly longing to do for years."

"Tip taught the children to waltz," marveled Willie, "and the children have taught their parents!"

"I believe that your brother Charlie will have a lot of fun in Puddling Center, Willie," said Professor Petit. He paused and a wistful expression came into his eyes. "Perhaps you, Willie—perhaps *you* will even prefer to remain in Puddling Center yourself. You haven't said what you thought of my plan for your future."

"Oh, no!" cried Willie. "I want to go with you and the dogs, Professor! I would like that more than anything else in the world. I'll make myself useful and learn all I can. I didn't answer you before because my heart was too full for words. I really could not *speak*!"

Sancho came and laid one paw affectionately upon Willie's knee.

"How are you, my friend?" he said. Willie laughed outright with pure pleasure.

"Very well, thank you, my friend," replied Willie. "I never felt better in all my life!"

The other dogs came and stood about Willie and wagged their tails. Grushenka tossed up her ball and Liddy stood on her hind legs. Prince rolled over and

Tip sat up to beg. Even the pony looked up from his buttercups and uttered a neigh of approval.

At that moment the stew boiled over, and Professor Petit said brisky: "Time to eat now, friends. The future will take care of itself."

# FURTHER READING

BY

# NANCY PEARL

If you enjoyed *The Highly Trained Dogs of Professor Petit*, you might like these books as well:

*The Incredible Journey* by Sheila Burnford
*Henry and Ribsy* by Beverly Cleary
*Love That Dog* by Sharon Creech
*Hurry Home, Candy* by Meindert DeJong
*The Giggler Treatment* by Roddy Doyle
*How to Steal a Dog* by Barbara O'Connor
*The 101 Dalmatians* by Dodie Smith
*The Case of Jack the Nipper* and sequels by H. L. Stephens
*A Dog on Barkham Street* by Mary Stolz
*A Dog Called Kitty* by Bill Wallace

# ABOUT THE AUTHOR

Carol Ryrie Brink (1895–1981) was an American author of more than thirty books for children and adults. She is widely known for her novel, *Caddie Woodlawn*, which won the 1936 Newbery Medal, the award given to the most distinguished contribution to American literature for children in a given year. Carol grew up in Idaho and later attended the University of Idaho. She transferred to the University of California, where she graduated Phi Beta Kappa in 1918. She married that same year and settled with her husband in St. Paul, Minnesota, where they lived for more than forty years and had two children. Brink's first novel, *Anything Can Happen on the River*, was published in 1934. Three of Brink's children's books are included in the Book Crush Rediscoveries series: *Family Grandstand* (1952), *Family Sabbatical* (1956), and *The Highly Trained Dogs of Professor Petit* (1953).

NANCY PEARL

PRESENTS

A BOOK CRUSH REDISCOVERY